Lolli Editions

Elastic

Original text © Johanne Bille, 2018
First published as *Elastik* by Forlaget Gladiator in Denmark, 2018
English translation © Sherilyn Hellberg, 2019
This English translation first published in Great Britain by Lolli Editions in 2019
1st edition, 1st impression

Design by Clara Birgersson
Typeset in Scala
Printed and bound by KOPA
Printed in Lithuania 2019

ISBN 978 1 9999928 0 4

DANISH ARTS FOUNDATION

Grateful acknowledgement is made to the Danish Arts Foundation
for supporting the translation of this book.

Lolli Editions would also like to thank the Consul George Jorck and
Wife Emma Jorck's Foundation.

A CIP catalogue record for this book is available from the British Library.

www.lollieditions.com

JOHANNE BILLE

ELASTIC

Translated by
Sherilyn Hellberg

I sit cross-legged in the shower and look at my vagina. I stretch my lips apart to see my clitoris and it's like looking at someone else, like I'm supposed to ask for permission before I touch it. I give up on shaving. There are too many folds down there and I don't like the folds. They're a curse, and I don't know how I'm supposed to feel about them or about the fact that I have a hole a penis can fill. I hate these pink curtains of flesh that have to be pulled aside first.

I dream of being manly. I dream that in the company of women I'm unlike them. I dream that my voice is hard and dark, that all my words sound important. Today, I think cunts are ugly.

Mathilde gave me a poster for my birthday. It slid out of her coat pocket and rolled onto the pavement as she was getting off her bicycle. I saw it happen from inside the café. She leaned over slightly and stretched her hand towards the pavement, not straining at all. Suddenly, the rolled-up poster was in her hand. It was still in her hand when she hugged me and said happy birthday. Gently, she pressed the roll of thick paper into my chest, and I could feel her knuckles against it, how my nipples stiffened and swelled. Mathilde didn't seem to notice. It's just a little something from me to you, she said. We were standing so close that the tips of our noses were almost touching, and I had to hold my breath to keep my balance, to avoid tipping over and pressing my nose into hers.

We sipped our coffees in the bright spring sun and I felt young and beautiful. My sunglasses fit the bridge of my nose perfectly, highlighting my cheekbones. I kept looking to the side so she would see my face in profile. Simon called from his office in Hanoi and said he wished he were there to give me a birthday kiss. You need a birthday kiss. You --- need one! The connection was bad. His voice crackled and I didn't tell him Mathilde's soft lips had already brushed against mine twice that day. A little tip of a tongue just barely touched my front tooth as her sunglasses clicked against mine.

Alexander points out a scrape on my knee I haven't noticed before, even though I usually notice that kind of thing, but I can't remember bumping my knee into anything or anything ever hurting. Do I have a cut? I ask. Alexander says yes, but it's not scabbed over yet. I should just let it be. We don't have sex that morning. He won't get hard. I tell him it's probably just because he's hungover, mostly so that he won't do anything about it, won't start touching himself or something. I like it when it's somewhere between soft and hard, that place in between. Not because of the challenge a half-erect penis can pose, but because it seems to be caught between two poles, like a ripple moving across the surface of the ocean.

Simon is reading the paper in the kitchen when I let myself in. The flakes of sunburn on his nose are the last trace of Hanoi's shower of sun rays. I open my laptop and google tides and ocean currents, but I don't find anything useful, and I suppose that's okay.

Autumn arrives and I drink one non-alcoholic beer after another while I wait for it to get dark outside. Fortunately, it's getting dark earlier and earlier. In a few weeks, I'll only have to drink a couple before the sun goes down and I can switch to normal beer. It's not that I want to get drunk. Actually, I'd rather be sober because I keep feeling like I'm losing track of things, but I've been having trouble eating. Food just doesn't taste like anything. So, I start drinking non-alcoholic beers as soon as I get back from work, but they're a paltry substitute. Simon tells me I smell like a bar. I just had one non-alcoholic beer, I lie. I don't understand what's going on with you lately, he said a few days ago. What do you mean? I said. Well, yesterday you were crying so much your whole body was shaking, and today you're laughing hysterically like you're high.

What's the problem then?

Simon keeps insisting we discuss my alcohol consumption

and mood swings. It all started when we moved into a bigger flat after he came back from Hanoi. One of the rooms is still empty because we don't have any furniture to put in it and Toke can't move in until next month. And now it's as if the empty room has to be filled up with all this conversation, to keep the silence from echoing between the walls. Or maybe it's the other way around: Simon's discontent – his feeling of being taken for granted – was always there, and now there's finally a designated space for him to store his anxiety. Why aren't you looking me in the eye? he says over and over, and I answer: I'm looking you in the eye right now, aren't I?

The door to the empty room won't close all the way. Something's wrong with the latch and it keeps creeping open like a stab in the back, and I don't like it. I hate living in a flat that keeps trying to give me away. I can feel the door slowly sliding open as soon as I turn my back to it.

Had these feelings been hiding under the surface all along like the moths in our rug? We didn't know they were there until we laid the rug down in the living room and they flew out, swarming towards the light. Their wings left greybrown stains on the walls. It happened overnight. Suddenly, the flapping creatures were everywhere. Simon whacked them to the floor with his open palm one after the other, squashing them with his soft slippers. He had to stamp on each one multiple times to kill it.

Our friends are having a dinner party. Usually I don't mind being around this particular group of people, but tonight it feels less like they're around me and more like they've surrounded me. Something has changed since the last time we were all together, but I don't know what. On the face of it, everything is the same as always: almost everyone standing in the kitchen, stirring a pot or affectionately grabbing each other by the shoulders. Saying things like: How long has it been? and: Let's do something soon! Everyone else is sitting around the dining room table, talking as fast as they can with engaged expressions to avoid taking part in the kitchen spectacle.

Now it's time for the eating ceremony and for the host to raise her glass and give her it's-so-wonderful-you-all-could-make-it-and-what-lovely-gifts-you-shouldn't-have speech. And then some silent chewing and cutlery against plates, bottles of beer opened and poured into glasses, and when the table is cleared and the Bezzerwizzer box opened, I'm still not having a good time. Simon shoots me a smile from the other side of the table. He winks like he always does in this kind of situation, and normally it's enough to make me laugh a little into my glass, but tonight the smile from the other side of the table isn't enough. Everyone sitting around the table is a zombie with vacant eyes and canned laughter, and I think I hate them. When we cycle home, I'm loud and sarcastic – rude – and I tell Simon that I know I'm being – rude – sorry. Still, I say: I can't go home right now. I'm too angry to go to bed.

He cycles through the junction without looking back and I take the metro to Nørreport. I stand there on Frederiks-borggade, looking around. I sit down on a bench, smoke half a cigarette and squash it with the heel of my boot until it stops glowing. I want to text Mathilde, but I can't figure out what to write. Instead I call Dina to convince her to come out for a beer, but she doesn't answer her phone. I walk to-wards Nørrebro, on the look-out for someone I might know, but all the faces I see are windblown and grim and even if I were to run into someone I probably wouldn't recognise them. Simon isn't asleep when I get in. He's lying in bed with his computer on his lap and he doesn't look up when I pull my dress over my head or throw my tights over the armchair. I lie down next to him in the glow of his screen and dream that Dina is having a baby that I want to kill as soon as it lands in my hands, covered in amniotic fluid, and half-awake half-dreaming I realise that I probably could kill a human being, and it actually feels like a valuable realisation. That I, at least in my dreams, have the nerve to do what needs to be done.

The morning after we had sex for the first time, a feeling of irrevocability festered in my body. A strange kind of backache, a stinging sensation in my vagina. The sky was glowing blue. The sunlight through the window lit up all the stains and flecks of dust, the traces of greasy fingers that had touched the glass at some point. I opened the balcony door and hid under the duvet again, rubbing Alexander's chest with stiff fingers until he finally woke up. Did I wake him up just to punish him? At least, I wanted to be sure that he knew I was irritated by the way he enunciated sentences like this one:

I want to fuck you right here.

I don't think this is that kind of bar, I said. What I really meant was that I couldn't care less what he wanted, but apparently I cared enough to kiss him, to flirt back. It's difficult to explain situations like these to Simon, even more so to justify why I didn't come home and snuggle up next to him under the blanket that night. Instead, I was rolling around on a kitchen table knocking over coffee mugs, and coffee from the afternoon made my hair smell warm and brown, tangled against my neck. It's also difficult to explain where all the bruises are coming from. My thighs and my knees are covered in bruises as big as fingers, and I press them down to make sure they all stay the same size. They're beautiful, Alexander says. Simon doesn't say anything, probably because he doesn't notice them.

For the last year, I've been planting a minefield of lies, which I now have to tiptoe carefully across. Strangely enough, I don't lie about the nights I spend with Alexander because Simon and I have agreed to tell each other if we have sex with other people, but that means I need to lie about something else. I tumble around in white lies about timing or my general behaviour, small things that neither provide nor avoid explanation: we cycled home around 2 a.m. (we took a cab at 4), I managed to get five hours of sleep (I slept for 45 minutes), I don't want to do it again (of course I do), and I'm just in an odd mood because I don't know what I want to do with my life.

When a film reaches its point of no return, no one acknowledges out loud that it has, but the audience knows, and the actors in the movie know too. It's the same with me, and yet, it's different. There isn't a single point of no return in this story. There's a series of them: a first one, then one for real, and so on.

Mathilde and I bought a can of coke to share and found our bench in Hans Tausen's Park. She had left her mittens at home so I lent her one of mine. We kept saying that life was beautiful, quietly reassuring each other that nothing was broken, that nothing had changed. Life is beautiful, we are beautiful, this is beautiful. I'm just happy that you and Alexander get along so well, she said, and I took a sip and passed her the can. She tipped her head back and emptied it with her eyes closed. It was like she disappeared a little in that moment. Already then, she was starting to disappear.

A year later, we are mere memories of each other, memories of an infatuation that never turned into more. A long, drawn-out hug goodbye that turned into a kiss. Her hands around my neck, mine on her lower back. That kiss was too close to love. She didn't dare turn around to say goodbye. She just spun on her heel and walked to her bicycle, fumbled with the lock, the pedals moving before her backside even hit the seat. I downed the last of my coffee and ran after her, just in time to see her disappear around the corner.

Simon doesn't know whether he's okay with it. The word *it* has taken on a new meaning for us. It's a code word for me sleeping with Alexander, a bad one because all the times we've had sex don't fit into one category, and yet. Might trick me once, I won't let you trick me twice, Kelis says. But Simon isn't Kelis. I don't know whether I'm okay with it, he says, and then he doesn't say anything else.

Maybe it would help if you guys had a beer together, I say, and Simon responds timidly that maybe it would. But it should be spontaneous, shouldn't it? he adds. I know that there's no such thing as spontaneous. I can only imagine the tense atmosphere, the two of them seated around an old wooden table at a bar. Simon wrapping his hands around his empty beer bottle, Alexander disappearing into the snow because he can't deal with the fact that the nights we've spent together mean something and maybe even have consequences. The nights that we, with our respective moans, assure each other don't mean anything. This sound is meaningless:

UUUUAAAOOOOOOHHH.

Toke moves in. On Sunday, he brings his bed, Monday his desk, and Tuesday a rug, and Simon and I can breathe a little easier. Finally, Toke is here, we're both thinking. I don't even need to ask. I can tell when Simon gives Toke a hug in the doorway. I hope that Toke will be our white dwarf. Our star has become too heavy. We can't keep carrying it by ourselves. A white dwarf in the system could be the solution. When a white dwarf star takes up matter from its neighbouring stars, it explodes in a supernova, and I imagine that our supernova will be our new beginning, that Toke moving in will take some of the load off – make it a little easier to exist. Toke has brought some beers to celebrate. Simon and I share one because Simon has football practice soon, and I'm supposed to be writing yet another application for a job that seems more interesting than my current one. That's how I justify my job search to Simon when he asks.

Now that Simon is gone, I spend most of my time on Facebook, watching *How I Met Your Mother* and clipping my toenails until there isn't anything left but cuticles and soft little lunulae. That's how January disappears. And I drink lots of sparkling water, that's also how January goes by, I drink sparkling water in greedy gulps, and the bubbles sting the inside of my nostrils and make my eyes water, and I imagine my restlessness pouring out of me, but there's always more restlessness inside. Stuck behind my eyeballs like a cold. Thick yellow slime.

Simon's coffee mug – the one with the broken handle – has been left by the sink, and I don't wash it. I just leave it on the counter with the imprint of his lips on the rim. You can't see it with the naked eye, but I can tell. The flat feels strange without his things in it. We packed them up carefully before he left and carried the moving boxes up to the attic and now they're waiting there, one floor above, to be moved to our new home when he returns.

I turn the cup around in my hands, letting the chipped

handle press against the pad of my thumb, and suddenly I see him standing right there next to me making coffee. Maybe he'll smoke a cigarette at the windowsill while the coffee runs through the machine. The smoke from his cigarette is white in the January night sky, and I get so angry that he's not actually here. Why didn't he say, come with me! Why did he leave me here with linens that don't smell like us anymore, empty space in the cupboard, and plants that will die because I give them too much water or not enough.

We didn't talk about it. There wasn't any reason to. He didn't want me to come. He had to do this on his own. He packed his suitcase on New Year's Day and disappeared down the stairs and I ran down after him and kissed him deeply in the stairwell. I kissed each of his cheeks, his eyebrows, his forehead, and then he started to cry, and I started crying too. I'll be home soon, he said, it's only six months. I'll be back before you know it. And I wiped my nose on my sleeve, and it was romantic like in the movies. I understand, I said, lying. This job is a once-in-a-lifetime opportunity, he said, mostly to himself. My fingers didn't want to let go. They were caught in his coat pockets and I could feel that he, in that moment, didn't really care about farmers' rights in Vietnam, that he would rather stay in our little flat with its poorly insulated windows and mould in the corners. See you soon, I said, and let go.

I don't have a burning desire to make a difference in the world or to do anything for anyone other than myself. I don't even know what I care about now that Simon is gone. I answer the office phone, prepare parcels for customers, wait for the postman, take the bus home. I sit in the corner of the sofa and my computer screen flickers in front of me as one episode of *How I Met Your Mother* slips into the next. I reach the fourth season, Stella says yes to Ted, and I feel nothing. Even a proposal can't make me feel something. Maybe my inability to care can be traced back to some untreated psychological disorder that I've had since I was little, and which is impossible to treat by this point. Maybe it's just boredom or that I'm dying faster than everyone else. Maybe my body is dying too fast and my brain is disintegrating, it can only handle its own basic survival and a few flickers of entertainment, brief moments of pleasure. I don't even have the energy to make myself smarter. I'm too impatient. I get distracted too easily. Maybe that's how I've always been. When I was a kid, I didn't take piano lessons or play handball after school. I played *The Sims* on my computer, controlling my Sims day after day. I planned and executed entire lives and it was pretty entertaining. At first, it was just the usual moves, like taking the ladder out of the pool and watching the poor Sims suffer a slow death, but the lives of my Sims soon became complicated. There were love triangles in shared houses, carefully planned birthday parties where it came out that someone was cheating in front of the other party guests, slaps in the face and fist fights. And my favourite: making a Sim do so many things at once that they would just go back and forth around the house without accomplishing a single task until, finally, they would shit their pants, set fire to themselves or collapse from exhaustion.

Eventually, I got tired of playing that kind of game, so I made Sims based on my friends and nemeses (mostly the latter) from school. It was wonderful to see Sim-Nikoline collapse from hunger in the kitchen and to start fights between the kids who teased me. I dreamed about *The Sims* at night. I would constantly hear the soundtrack, the eternal cling-clanging of electronic music, playing on a loop. Some nights, it still rings in my ears. It's a unique tinnitus that I don't dare tell anyone about.

There was something different about her.

That's how it all started. A dried bit of sleep was caught on one of her short, greyish eyelashes, and the little, bright speck moved up and down when she blinked. Eventually, it dropped from her eyelash and landed on her flushed cheek. It was freezing outside. Soon, March. I felt the urge to softly brush the little speck away with my finger, but I resisted. Alice, meet Mathilde – your new colleague, my boss said. She offered her hand in an assured way, her fingers cold and bony, but maybe they were just numb from outside. She quickly undid the big buttons of her winter coat and threw it over the chair closest to her, sitting down next to it. She rubbed her hands together a little desperately, and I wanted to wrap my hands around them, to squeeze them and transfer my warmth to her.

I remember the first time I met Mathilde. In that sense, she's different from everyone else I've ever been in love with, but I can't remember the next few times I saw her, so she's also different in that way. It must have been at the office. We sat across from each other, our desks mirrored. We could catch each other's eyes by looking up from our computer screens and leaning a bit to the side. I'd come home tired every day, but in a good way. I would hoover and wash the floors, drinking a glass of wine in the kitchen while the floors dried. It took a long time. It rained every day and nothing in the flat ever seemed to dry completely. Everything was tinged with moisture.

The wet laundry hanging in the bedroom and living room only increased the level of humidity. I couldn't stop cleaning. It felt necessary after the six seasons of *How I Met Your Mother* I had watched in January. All this housework was more than a diversion. Cleaning had become meditative for me in a way that practical tasks had never been before: slowly dusting shelves with a wet rag and picturing the little speck of dried goo on her eyelash, methodically hoovering the floors and imagining big, round buttons pried out of their holes by stiff fingers and chewed nails.

At ten o'clock, I fell asleep in clean sheets and slept a dreamless sleep. I woke up around seven, got out of bed and pulled a dress down from the clothes rack. Found a cardigan in the drawer. I think all of February went by like that. Maybe something inside me knew that I wouldn't want to spend my time cleaning a few months from now? Like a bear going into hibernation, I isolated myself in my little hole. I was preparing for the coming of summer, its ravenous consumption of nourishment. I was lying in wait, but I wasn't even waiting – not really. Bears probably don't wait for summer and its abundance of food, and they don't sleep because they want to. They wake up because their instinct, their biological clock, tells them it's time.

I woke up in March.

It wasn't abrupt like you see in the movies. When the camera zooms in on the face of the person waking, and BOOM! their eyes open. I awoke slowly, disoriented. It took days for me to understand what was happening. It bothers me now, that I let my feelings for Mathilde sneak up on me like that.

We were sitting at the bar, or rather, Mathilde had taken a seat at the bar that first night, and when I arrived, I thought she wasn't there. I stood in the doorway looking for her among all the other talking, drinking, smoking people, and my stomach clenched. And then a delicate, pale hand waved. There she was, smiling from one of the high bar stools, but not like we were colleagues, more like we knew each other's deepest secrets. We talked a bit about work, about our plans for the weekend. But it wasn't the usual small talk, at least not the kind I was used to. I raised my beer bottle to my lips, but Mathilde stopped me: In this bar, we use glasses. Even though I prefer to drink from the bottle too, she said as her hand brushed my thigh.

Was it a date?

There was a little space between us as we drank our first beer. A woman sat down next to me and hung a boxy bag over her chair. It kept bumping into my knee, but it didn't bother me. I just pushed my chair closer to Mathilde's. The woman with the bag bought a round and winked at me. Why should it matter whether you're born with a dick or a cunt? Mathilde said. She lit another cigarette and talked about emancipation and stigma. Her voice was strong in a way I hadn't heard before. Suddenly, I felt light and airy. Her words were like hundreds of helium balloons tied to my feet, my knees, my shoulders, my ears. My plaited hair.

I don't regret anything I've done, Mathilde said, because I'm happy to be where I am now. A droplet of beer clung to her upper lip as the words came out. I could feel with my entire body that I was younger than her. That I still had my youth, that hers was disappearing, ebbing away.

I slept with her.

Mathilde nodded towards the bartender. It was only a few times, just because, you know. And I made a noise that indicated that I knew.

Back home, I'm restless and you're skyping me from Hanoi and saying that you can't sleep, that you miss me, that six

34

months is too long to be apart. I feel a bubbling feeling and say I love you too. It's dark in your room and I can only see the outline of your face when you hold up the phone close to your eyes, which makes you squint a little. Something has changed. I was so jealous of you and your adventures when you were sending me pictures of palm trees and penthouses and gin & tonics. Now it's the other way around. I send you pictures of Copenhagen bursting in the spring, and you send me long messages about how much you're looking forward to coming home and going on adventures together in our city, the same Copenhagen that you, a few months ago, couldn't stand. That feeling is apparently gone. Or you're starting to realise that your dissatisfaction with everything besides me might have more to do with yourself than where you are.

You don't want to hang up. My thumb hovers over the red button on the screen as you, for a second time, ask what I'm doing tomorrow. I'm so tired, I say, and you smile and give the camera a kiss. Your lips fill the screen. Finally you hang up and my hands are free. My fingers press against my clitoris in the way that usually works, but the pictures in my head appear in flashes, and my clit and my wrist start hurting, but my fingers keep going.

I inherited my dad's greed. It's there in my breasts and my belly and my cunt. In the gap between my front teeth which has gotten smaller with age but is still big enough to fit a string of spaghetti through. My greed is impossible to get rid of. It laughs mockingly at me in the mirror. You can try your best to be virtuous, it says, but I'm stuck inside you. Like the genetic mutation that causes breast and cervical cancer. Angelina Jolie has it. She had a mastectomy and hysterectomy. They call it risk-reducing surgery. I can't prevent the consequences though. My greed is just there, destroying everything.

My greed and boredom are intertwined, strung together inside my body. As a teenager, I learned that addiction was the only thing that could relieve my greed and boredom, and alcohol was sitting right there. Being drunk for the first time was wonderful. My world was turned upside down, I was in free fall. When I was sixteen years old, I got so drunk I peed my pants outside the front door of my childhood home. The complete loss of control was fantastic. Listening to my own urine splashing on the pavement, completely alone with that sound and the warm feeling between my legs, spreading across my buttocks. After that night, there was no going back. I waited in line to get into nightclubs with my fake ID and lied with hungry eyes about my age, my star sign, my home address. Anything was possible. No one noticed I was spiralling. Or they didn't care. Was my obsession with alcohol a conscious choice?

My obsession with Mathilde wasn't.

Most women I know provoke a sense of powerlessness in me, combined with a mild discomfort. Sometimes, especially at night, I enjoy the company of certain women, select women, women I've decided to keep in my life because I like the way they empty a beer. Or the way they puff on their cigarette and casually stub it out with a lazy, indifferent movement of their hand. The cigarette smoulders in the ashtray as though they've neglected to properly finish its life. It just lies there glowing with smudged lipstick on the orange filter. Usually I smother it. Calmly, I fish the butt up out of the ashtray and crush it until the smoke disappears. I notice a little smudge of red from the lipstick on the tip of my finger. It feels intimate. Like being alone in the house of someone you don't really know. I wait until she gets distracted by something: a change in the music or someone coming through the door. Once, one of them caught me in the act. She abruptly stopped talking and asked: Why did you do that? I couldn't give her an answer. I couldn't explain my behaviour, why the smoke bothered me.

I have a hard time with women, which is another reason why my feelings for Mathilde catch me by surprise. Suddenly she's taken over my life. I turn off my phone in the evening to keep myself from constantly checking whether she's written or responded or is online, but I turn it back on minutes later. It starts with the evenings, but soon she takes my nights too. One night, she sends me a message at three in the morning, and I wake up and respond. She sends me a message at the same time the next night, and I wake up and respond again. The following night, I wake up at three in the morning on my own, staring expectantly at my phone until a little red heart pops up. An emoji blowing a kiss. Goodnight.

I have an especially hard time with women who call themselves my *girl* friends. I had my first encounter with female friendship in primary school. That was when the discomfort started. I remember rollerblading with Laura. We would go rollerblading every day in the car park the summer before year six. There was an asphalt ramp at one end and it wasn't meant for rollerblades, but it was perfect. We flew down the ramp with our plaits flapping in the air, and with cramped thighs we fought our way back up again. It was worth it. The rush of letting ourselves glide down the ramp with the wind in our hair was worth the pain. The feeling of flying. We spent that summer tottering up and riding down, entire afternoons. We also talked a lot, but I can't remember any of our conversations. They were probably just the kind of conversations kids have about asphalt and knee pads. How they crumpled our jeans around the knees, leaving our skin wrinkled and red. Our parents insisted that we wear knee pads. It felt like a fair price to pay in exchange for all those happy days in the car park. When school started again, Nikoline invited Laura over to her house, and then they bought the same green top from Nørgaard Paa Strøget. They were sitting next to each other like two green street lights when I walked into the classroom with my rollerblades tied to my rucksack. Laura didn't have to say anything. The matching tops said it all.

Year seven was all about friendship necklaces. A silver heart, broken in half. You were supposed to wear it around your neck under your top. A half heart against warm kid's skin. It meant that you belonged to someone, that you had a best friend. The half heart on the chain was proof. Who has the other half, we would ask each other, who's your best friend? I didn't have a friendship necklace because no one gave me their other half, and I didn't have half a heart to give to anyone because my parents thought it was ridiculous to spend so much money on what was clearly just a trend. But it wasn't just a trend. Those friendship necklaces were life or death, they determined your survival. I couldn't convince my parents, but I also couldn't let on that I cared. Nikoline and Laura bought theirs at the jewellery shop next to school. I remember Nikoline dramatically ripping the chain off her neck and throwing it at Laura. You're the worst friend in the world, she screamed. Laura walked home from school in tears with her half silver heart burning against her breastbone. I thought that we were finished with girl problems after those friendship necklaces. But apparently my problems with *girl* friends were only just beginning.

Friendship between women is, for the most part, invisible, and is only revealed in furtive glances and demonstrated leniency in regards to who paid for the last coffee and who will pay for the next. Friendship between women is like scaffolding. Everyone knows scaffolding is temporary but necessary if you want to restore the façade of a house. But no one keeps scaffolding up indefinitely, no matter how solid it seems. All scaffolding gets taken down, and female friendships get taken down too. Some hold out for a while and make it through a few windy Sundays, hurricane-strength gusts. Others are taken down as quickly as they were put up.

Is Mathilde my *girl* friend if I'm in love with her?

What happened those first few months?

A lot, but also not much at all. There were a lot of Skype calls to Hanoi, and then there weren't so many anymore. There were some beers at Café Intime, and then there were more. I remember them. I remember each and every beer. I remember all of Mathilde's beers, that I paid for them because Mathilde was always broke, Mathilde and Alexander were always broke. It wasn't just the two of us that first night either. Alexander arrived a few hours later, and when he walked through the door, all conversation came to a halt, as though someone had pressed pause. Beer stopped fizzing in everyone's glasses. All eyes were drawn to their slim bodies, their kiss. Again that clench in my stomach, the moisture. Sweat and tears and fog. Damp.

Something else in me too when he walked through the door, something that was released by the way he pulled out the bar stool. It wasn't the same as the bubbling feeling I had around Mathilde, it was milder, an undercurrent of sorts.

An echo. My feelings were finally able to materialise, taking the shape of this tall, beautiful human I had to have. I want what Mathilde has, I want to own it, possess it. Isn't that the ultimate form of love? From that very first night, I knew I was going to fuck Alexander, that I would have to love him.

Alexander and Mathilde talked at length about the prison of monogamy. They kept touching each other as they talked, and I kept nodding, demonstrating my agreement without saying a word. With every nod, they continued. They told me about how they, years ago, had climbed an elm tree to be closer to the stars. You lost one of your shoes, remember? Alexander laughed and said he remembered. He also remembered how nervous he'd been when deciding he couldn't keep his secret to himself any longer, and, high on MDMA and stardust, had said:

I cheated on you.
I cheated on you too.

They got married. It was a marriage in protest. They invited all their lovers to the reception. Their parents and grandparents, aunts and uncles went around introducing themselves to all these lovers. What sweet friends you both have, what a nice bunch of young people, they said. I can see it now: the two newlyweds giggling like naughty children. Mathilde in her short white dress and Alexander in his slightly oversized suit. All dressed up, ready for the show.

Why did you get married?

It's all part of the project, they said in unison. They talked over each other in their eagerness to share the importance of free love and honesty, of life without jealousy or possessiveness. When I returned to the table with another round, they were devouring each other. I could barely make out the contours of the bridge their tongues had built between their faces. They look like each other, I thought. I wanted to look like them too. If only there were room for my tongue. And then the bridge collapsed. Their faces drew apart and Alexander said cheers, Mathilde too:

To art!
Cheers to the art project!
Cheers to love!

I can't figure out how to describe what's been happening the last few months, but Simon needs an explanation. When he pops up on my screen, he smiles and winks, but in a way that indicates he knows something fundamental has changed. For one, he knows that I'm not bored anymore. I'm not sending him texts about silly things or constantly telling him how much I miss him. It's not because I don't love him anymore. It's not about him, it's about other people. It's never been about other people before, it's always been about us. He's the sun I revolve around and then suddenly he isn't. My connection to him has broken. There are many black holes in this story, there are a lot of things I can't explain or justify. I forget our Skype dates and send messages to apologise a few hours later, my texts brief and full of typos. Were you drunk? Simon asks.

It doesn't have anything to do with being drunk. I don't think so anyway, except that alcohol doesn't make it easier to come up with a good excuse for why I'm suddenly forgetting our Skype dates, forgetting him. I tell him about the new people in my life, about our nights at the brown bars, but I can't convey how completely they consume me, how time and everyone else disappears when I'm around them. I don't actually enjoy talking to Mathilde and Alexander, listening to them talking to each other. I never listen to what they're saying. I just watch their lips change shape, becoming channels of sound. It's like how I don't like the taste of beer or cigarettes but still want to drink and smoke. We didn't laugh in our drunkenness. We looked at each other, grazing each other's legs under the table. A hand on a sleeve. Were you drunk? Simon asks. No, I wasn't drunk, I was befuddled. I can't explain the difference to him.

I remember one *girl* friend, a friendship that ended before it began. Her name was Tanja, Tanja my short-lived *girl* friend with a big mane of black hair gathered together in a tight ponytail that swung from side to side even when she was sitting still. One day, on the way home from school, we sat together because there happened to be two free seats next to each other on the metro. It was the first time we ever talked, even though we went to the same parties and saw each other every day at lunch. We talked about all kinds of things. We had kissed the same guy, apparently, and both of us thought that he was an idiot. It was a good start to a first conversation that would also be the last. Tanja told me her deepest secret – I've never had an orgasm – and suggested we live together when we started at university in the autumn. It's so soon, she said. Her dad wanted to buy her a flat in Vesterbro, and I could move in before the semester started in August, and we could drink wine on weeknights and talk about our jobs, jobs that would be time-consuming and draining but also really grown-up. I want to be a nurse, Tanja said. I want to work in the children's cancer unit at Rigshospitalet. That's the dream, don't you think, devoting your life to helping others. I agreed because I wanted Tanja to be my friend. It had something to do with her shiny ponytail.

Tanja and I didn't end up becoming friends, even though she gave me her phone number and we hugged each other goodbye. She typed the numbers into my phone and left a heart after her name in case there were other Tanjas in my contacts. There weren't and there aren't. Tanja <3 is still in my phone. I saw her in the school canteen the next day and her ponytail was swinging from side to side with more force than usual. We won't be friends after all, it seemed to be saying. She's having a baby, the announcement pops up in my newsfeed, and even though our friendship didn't last long I'm happy for her when I see the grainy grey picture of a foetus as big as a plum.

Morten joins us at Café Intime one night. He's just come back from Portugal. He's been in exile, he adds, and I ask him what he means, and he says that it's because of them, Mathilde and Alexander, and nods in their direction. Outside the wind is blowing sheets of rain at frail bodies and ripping umbrellas apart but inside the bar is thick with smoke. Mathilde and Alexander's faces have a greyish glow, and it looks good on them, even that looks good on Alexander and Mathilde. They'll chew you up and spit you out, Morten says, you'll become a sad little clump, and it will be their fault, and they'll say poor you, and then they won't want to be around you anymore because you don't have your shit together. Make sure you don't fall in love with them, he says, you have to keep your shit together. I don't tell Simon about Morten's warning. I tell him I took the train home early, that the night was windy and eventless.

I'm on the train to Škofja Loka. It's an escape, this trip, a well-planned escape. I started making plans after I kissed Mathilde for the first time, and I booked the flight one morning when the screen of my phone remained black, lonely without a message from her. Why are you going to Slovenia, Simon asked, and I couldn't tell him the truth. I need to get away from Copenhagen, I need to get away from Mathilde's short eyelashes. Instead I told him: I need to experience something new. Simon frowned, his eyebrows drawn together. His face was pixelated on the computer screen, but I could sense him trying to make out my expression from his office in Hanoi. It's probably good for you to take a break from Copenhagen, he said.

According to my ticket I'll arrive in Škofja Loka at 4.12 p.m., but I want to stay on the train and let myself be taken forward without going anywhere. There's something liberating about sitting on a quiet train watching the hills and trees sailing by, feeling the distance between Mathilde and me grow, the green repeatedly interrupted by a noisy river. The rivers are full of meltwater because it's spring and I've read that this is the best time of year to experience the Slovenian landscape. The window frames the forests and the treetops look jubilant, as if each branch is an arm raised overhead in the ecstasy of spring.

Tomaž is supposed to pick me up at the station and even though I've told him that I won't get there until 5 p.m., he's standing there waiting for me when the train rolls into the station on time. He seems annoyed that I lied about my arrival time and tells me in a quiet voice that he had to ask the people in the ticket booth when my train was getting in, that he was worried I had taken the wrong train. But now you're here! he says suddenly, almost triumphantly, I'll show you the apartment you'll be staying in. The flat is close to the train station and Tomaž carries my big blue rucksack on one shoulder, pointing at things as he tells me about them. That's McDonald's, he says, and down there by the river is the library.

I'm not staying with Tomaž. I'm staying in Žiga's flat, but he's in Croatia visiting his girlfriend – that's why Tomaž is picking me up. I look forward to meeting you in a few days, Žiga has written hastily on a piece of paper waiting on the dining table. Next to the note, there's a USB stick with the first three seasons of *The Bridge* on it. In case you feel homesick, he's written. But I'm not homesick. I'm relieved. There's no one to tell.

WELCOME TO ARTIST QUARTER is written over the entrance to a little courtyard, surrounded by low-rise buildings and artists' studios. A bar called Ko Uciri in the middle of the courtyard pumps out lemonade and beer like a pulsing heart. Graffitied walls bear messages and slogans – *make art fight the system* – and I walk through a door that's slightly ajar and leads into a room full of furniture draped in white sheets. The walls are lined with paintings of a man with drooping eyes like he's just woken up. So many nearly identical faces, his sleepy gaze. His jawline resembles Simon's, but his eyebrows are bushy, dark like Mathilde's, and I hurry into the next room. A large mural with butterflies and a penis painted with hurried smudged blue brushstrokes. In the last room, a bar built from cardboard boxes and mannequins with broken skulls. Suddenly, I realise that a man is standing behind me. He has a single long, thin dreadlock, it's sticking out of the sleeve of his T-shirt. It follows his arm as he moves, snaking lazily along his skin. She's a little eccentric, the artist, he says, and I remember that I've met him before, he owns the studio in the back corner of the courtyard. He could have been anyone, I forget his face as soon as he turns the other way. Nonetheless, this is the only face I end up remembering in this city. This is the face that greets me in the supermarket, in the café by the city square, in the passageways behind the church. His name is Tomaž, this artist is called Tomaž too. The theme of the exhibition is *home* he says, *what is home to you*. What does that have to do with broken skulls, I ask, and Tomaž laughs hoarsely and lights a cigarette, a Marlboro Light, so at least I know that about him. This Tomaž smokes Marlboro Lights. But all of the other Tomažes do too, I soon find out.

I wake up after Žiga. He gets up around 8 a.m. and boils water for his herbal tea and eats some kind of cooked oats on top of yoghurt. I lie silently in bed listening to the sound of his spoon scraping against the edge of the bowl. I get up after he leaves and walk with sleepy eyes down to the supermarket because the bread in the local bakery is dry and expensive. The cashier knows what I want, she's a young girl with dark circles around her eyes, and she puts a croissant in a white bag and a loaf of bread in a dark bag. It's a small, thin loaf with salt and cumin on top, glistening with olive oil. A little further down the street is Zvezda Kafe where four actors waiting for their big break serve coffee and wink invitingly at passers-by. A double espresso and a freshly squeezed orange juice are placed in front of me. I don't even need to order, they already know what I drink every morning.

I'm a foreigner in this city, and my foreignness is reflected back at me in the puddles, the river, the polished windows of the library. The library is new and like me it doesn't fit in with the rest of the city. It was difficult to obtain planning permission to build it. There wasn't much public support for the project because the residents of Škofja Loka were fond of the old library with its worn-down charm and weren't interested in having it replaced by a new building. A small group of townspeople with cardboard signs and whistles assembled in the city square early one Friday morning, but the protest was useless. The building project was approved, and now there's a new library with clean lines and straight walls, and it never ends, Žiga says. Modernity has arrived and it's here to stay. He takes a deep breath and places his open hand on the concrete wall as if he's trying to dissolve it. A new concrete bridge with steel wires runs across the river in front of us, and on the other side of the bridge there's a new park with a little gazebo in the centre, where there were supposed to be nice little concerts on warm summer nights. Apparently, there was only one concert last summer. A band played some Slovenian classics, Žiga says.

I walk down the pedestrian street with my laptop bag hanging on one shoulder and my shoulder bag balanced on the other. All of the Tomažes stare at me, at the foreign body. They stare with eyes that aren't exactly unfriendly, but they aren't welcoming either. I can feel their gaze on my body like ticks crawling into my warm armpits and sinking their crawling legs into my skin, sucking on the foreign body. There's a wall between us, maybe because they're almost all named Tomaž and I'm not. I can't tell them apart. For me, they're all the same, in the way that different varieties of apples are always just apples at the end of the day. When you think about an apple, it's not like you have a Cox Orange or Ingrid Marie or Pink Lady in mind. It's only when you're at the greengrocer's, standing in front of piles of round fruits, that you start to think about the fact that there are different varieties of apples. One Tomaž is a composer. He gets struck by waves of inspiration and disappears for days, then reappears with red eyes and hollow cheeks. In the meantime, the other Tomažes drink espresso out of big, white cups and smoke pack after pack of Marlboro Lights. They pull their chairs towards the sunlight, squinting. They've been doing it for years. I can tell by the skin around their eyes, wrinkled from their chronic squinting.

My boyfriend is in Vietnam, I repeat again and again, I have to skype with my boyfriend in Vietnam, but the Tomažes don't seem to care at all. The bill is already paid, the bartenders and baristas and waiters say, this Tomaž or that Tomaž has already paid for you. I don't have the chance to say thank you because the Tomažes are always occupied, talking or smoking. One morning I stand slightly hidden behind a big potted plant and I watch them sitting in the sun. Finally, I can tell them apart. One stands out from the rest, the fine lines around his eyes suit him. He's skinny like a daddy longlegs and his broad forehead and almost provocatively beautiful features remind me of Alexander. The way he's smoking right now, as if he's a little surprised every time the filter hits his lips, regretting it as soon as the smoke enters his lungs. Mathilde never regrets smoking. I can tell by the way she closes her eyes when she lights her cigarette and takes the first drag. She sits like that for a while, with the cigarette in the corner of her mouth and smoke in her lungs, eyes closed.

Women come and go, the Tomažes tell me one night, but usually, they go. They stay for three months and then they disappear. There's a sense of sorrow in their acknowledgement, latent in the word *disappear*: They don't move, they don't travel to another city, they just disappear. But now *you're* here, the beautiful Tomaž says, and the other Tomažes nod and say in unison, Alice is here! And they cheer and smile and ask me again: How do you say cheers in Denmark? *Skål*, I say, trying to make my voice sound a little deeper, to make a gruff noise with my throat, or at least remove a bit of the femininity given away by my thighs, my elbows, my breasts. My dresses are balled up in my rucksack, I only wear baggy jeans and striped T-shirts.

I live in a flat full of Tomažes and an almost panicked sense of frustration about the futility of their lives hangs in the air. Aggression colours their relationships to each other like a string of lights. Red orange violet blue, violet again.

I have a fever and I cough deep inside my chest. No phlegm comes out, only the stench of sickness. My body doesn't belong in Škofja Loka, I realise, waking up in my sticky sheets. The fever has kicked me in the heart, and my heart is beating away, trying to outrun it. Am I going to die of a heart attack, I wonder as I dial the Danish emergency services on my phone and a recorded voice lets me know I'm number 10 in line. The nurse who answers my call tells me that it would be wise to look up the nearest hospital. She asks about my alcohol consumption and I tell her. She asks how many units a week, and then, more decisively, she says: Find the nearest hospital and ask for a blood test. It sounds like the flu, but just to be on the safe side. It might also be glandular fever. I want to tell her that it can't be glandular fever because Mathilde's kiss was too brief. Her saliva couldn't have mixed with mine.

I send a message to the oldest Tomaž, the one who actually goes by Tuzi, saying that I have a high temperature and think it could be glandular fever. I don't want to bother

61

you, I write, but do you know where the nearest hospital is? It sounds forced, I know I'm bothering him, that he'll now have to take me to the hospital.

The emergency ward has been moved to a new building, and Tuzi has to ask for directions twice before we're standing in front of the counter waving my EU health insurance card. Tuzi and the nurse raise their eyebrows. A series of questions and Tuzi confirms confidently: Vietnam. An alarm sounds and the nurses rush in. They run towards me in flapping white coats, and I try to explain that there's been a misunderstanding, that Tuzi's English isn't good enough, that my boyfriend lives in Vietnam, not me, but the alarm is so loud that the nurses can't hear me, or they don't want to, and I'm herded into a quarantined area. Doctors in white suits and masks check on me every half hour. Don't be afraid, they say. Up on the ceiling, there's a small, white speaker. Lukas Graham is playing on the radio. *Mama said that it was okay.*

Tuzi ran the other way when the nurses pushed me into the quarantined area. He ran to the door, which made me paranoid. Is there some kind of conspiracy I don't know about, does someone want me put away in solitary confinement? I think of all the Tomažes and their gingivitis grins when I met them that first day. Am I going to die in this hospital? Who wants me dead? A sneaking suspicion of a married couple in Copenhagen conspiring, a Simon in Hanoi deciding not to answer my calls.

I curl up on two plastic chairs and imagine spending the rest of my life here with the hazmat suits as my only friends. In *Independence Day*, a spaceship crashes into Earth and the humans find three aliens inside and lock them up. No, two of them are already dead from the crash, but one survives and is subjected to experiments and questioning. You don't see the experiments, but you know they hurt. Then this last alien dies, spread open on the operation table, surrounded by scientists in white coats. The three dead aliens swirling in cylindrical tanks in Area 51. I'm an alien too and I'm going to die in this Slovenian village. Who wants me dead? Everyone wants me dead because I'm not like everyone else, and they need to cut open my body to understand how a creature like me breathes, eats, sleeps. Dies. Strangely, for the first time since Mathilde opened those big buttons with her shaking cold fingers, I accept the state of things. I've been wondering how I ended up here, but it all makes sense now.

Every night, the Tomažes sing songs about me. They loudly recount my hospital visit, telling and retelling the story, even though I've barely told them anything. The story is expanding, I can tell that they'll be entertaining themselves with it for the next decade. I'm part of the group now, or at least, I'm not a guest anymore. Now we have a story in common, even though Tuzi ran the other way as soon as they started pushing me into quarantine. After eight hours, the nurses and doctors realised that there had been a misunderstanding, that I wasn't carrying some contagious East-Asian virus, and they wrote me a prescription for some painkillers and let me go. In a feverish fog, I found my way back to the flat and ran a bath. It took a long time, and when I finally slid into the warm water, the hot water tank next to the bathtub was happily grumbling. I found a face mask from the hospital in my trouser pocket. I kept taking it off and the nurses kept replacing it with a new one, pulling the elastic band around my ears, and the smell of the hospital disappeared, replaced by my sick breath. A nurse-in-training stuck a long

64

cotton bud up my nose, and I cried, shaking, and strong hands held me down and dry mouths kept telling me that I was *cool*, that the worst would be over soon.

The Tomažes say *danka*, laughing. It's the Slovenian word for Dane, as far as I understand, but apparently it sounds like another Slovenian word I don't know. I don't know why they're laughing. *Danka, danka!* they shout with big open mouths, pointing at my arse. You understand? One of them, slurring, says: Do you have music in Denmark? Roxette, the beautiful Tomaž answers for me. And I say yes yes. My phone buzzes in my pocket. It's Mathilde: Are you okay? How does Mathilde know I'm not okay? She must know, otherwise she wouldn't have texted. And the courtyard with its strings of lights and wicker chairs and graffiti on the walls turns into a stage, and the Tomažes become meaningless pieces of furniture. Only the message on my screen matters. I answer: Yes, but I miss you.

I miss you too!

And I feel a gentle tug on my plait, Mathilde grasping it from Copenhagen.

The beautiful Tomaž takes me to a vineyard a little outside Škofja Loka. He hasn't been there before either, so we turn on the GPS, which tells us to take a right and then a left. We climb the mountain in hairpin turns, and I have to hold onto my seatbelt and look at the road ahead of us to keep myself from throwing up. Tomaž puts on some old Slovenian pop, sticking his finger in the air like he's at a disco, first with his right hand, then his left. This song makes me nostalgic, he says. It's from an old movie. My phone buzzes in my pocket again. Mathilde is sending me pictures from the office, selfies, she's blowing kisses with big eyes. I take a picture of the view through the front window and she responds that she wishes she were here with me. Let's go somewhere together next time, she writes. Come home soon, she writes in another message. Tomaž is quiet. The song is over. Who's texting you? he asks. Nobody, I answer.

My conversations with Tomaž take place in fragments. He starts to say something and I finish the sentence for him. His English is the same as the other Tomažes' broken school

English, and he often stumbles, smiling and gesturing for me to help him find the right word, to fill in his sentences until they make sense. He wasn't interested in the story about the hospital. He laughed distractedly when one of the other Tomažes told yet another version of it. He disappeared, then reappeared with two beers, placing one of them on the table in front of me. Later, he put his hand on my thigh and I didn't push it away because it was as though his big hand was washing off the imprint of Mathilde's fingers.

He starts: We've only been driving for fifteen minutes and now it's like we're... In a different world, I finish for him. He turns the wheel with unnecessary force. Do you want to go to a wine tasting? he asked me yesterday. We can ask the others if they want to come. Nobody wanted to, but he called me the next morning anyway, ready to go, and I hurried down to the courtyard, waiting impatiently in the midday sun, smoking a cigarette, and then another. Finally, he showed up in the low doorway to his studio, squinting a little as he took his car keys out of his pocket.

Where have you been?

I was painting, he said, but I don't believe him because he doesn't have a model. He talks about it every morning. If only I could find a model, he says, then I could start painting again. *If only I could find one.* And I laugh, shaking my head, involuntarily high-pitched as if to camouflage my refusal.

The next morning he says the same thing, shaking a sachet of cane sugar and mumbling something about a model, and then he empties the little packet into his espresso, almost stirring and drinking it at the same time.

I need a model, Tomaž says again today. The sentence is part of our morning routine. We meet in the courtyard, order our espressos and spread out in wicker chairs looking at each other, our faces still rumpled with sleep. Then I say that it's warm today or there's rain in the forecast, and Tomaž says that he needs a model. He lights his first cigarette of the day, looks around the courtyard with wrinkled eyebrows and then exclaims: Roadtrip! One more adventure, just the two of us. He stubs his cigarette out in his empty glass and we walk in silence towards the car park to the rundown car which he never locks. If you get tired of living with Žiga, he says, you can always sleep in my car. He has a distant look in his eyes, a combination of love and contempt. For what? This place, the stagnation, the identical days, the same conversations on repeat. Himself, maybe. Probably just himself.

He opens the car door. He puts on Coldplay. *We're going out into the world*, he keeps saying as he presses down on the accelerator and the car moves forward in jerks.

There's a chocolate festival in Radovljica and Tomaž

looks out of place among the families with children and chocolate boxes in paper bags. He looks out of place in most places besides Škofja Loka. I can see it when he orders two soft drinks at the small café in the town square. He's out of place in Radovljica, but to me it looks the same as Škofja Loka. The only difference is that the roads are a little hillier, it's closer to the Alps. Look at Triglav, he says pointing ahead. You can't see it, but it's there behind the clouds.

You cannot see it but you can.
Amazing.

Chocolate on folding tables, neatly arranged pralines on silver platters. The sun moves slowly across the sky, its rays slide over one booth and then move on to the next, and the chocolate turns soft, glistening in the heat before congealing in the shade. Cocoa butter crystallises in grey blotches. We walk in silence through the crowd. Tomaž buys a bar of chocolate and offers me a piece. One more, you need it. It's milk chocolate with crushed pumpkin seeds. This is the taste of Slovenia, he says with a speck of pumpkin seed stuck in the corner of his mouth. Our tongues turn green from pumpkin seed dust. There's pumpkin seed dust all over my hands, and I wipe them on my trousers, ready to let my fingers intertwine with Tomaž's.

Tomaž asks if I would like to go to his sister's for lunch. I haven't had an actual conversation with one single woman in this town, and I'm tempted by the thought of having another woman around. Someone who can tell me about this place, someone who can tell me about all the Tomažes and their monotonous lives. Maybe she'll be like Mathilde. His sister lives outside the city in one of the housing developments that was built when Slovenia was still part of Yugoslavia. They're everywhere: houses with small, square windows and thick walls with dusty red and yellow accents. She has a cat and a dog, Tomaž says. You're not afraid of dogs, are you? I tell him I'm not, that I'm more afraid of cats than dogs. I hate their unpredictable eyes and sharp claws grabbing at my long hair and jumper sleeves.

Tomaž's sister isn't a kindred spirit. She's an old woman with melancholy eyes. She rummages around a basket in the hallway and hands me a tattered pair of slippers, nodding at my shoes. Tomaž tells me that this is a custom in Slovenia homes: We welcome with slippers. They're too big and I have to slide across the floor to avoid stepping out of them.

She's made a gloopy bean dish which she shovels onto plastic plates. In the middle of the table, there's a bowl of iceberg lettuce and pumpkin seed oil. We eat the salad straight out of the bowl. Tomaž impales a few large leaves with his fork and forces them into his mouth so they crack and liquid squirts all over the tablecloth. The dog is a black cocker spaniel. First, it begs for food from Tomaž's sister, then Tomaž, and then me. A little black paw on my thigh and a pair of soft eyes with white eyelashes. Tomaž's sister doesn't say anything and Tomaž chatters away, crunching his salad. He asks questions that his sister answers with a nod or by shaking her head. Ronja, she says suddenly, pointing at the dog, Astrid Lindgren.

When we get up to leave, there's still a lot of salad left in the large bowl, and Tomaž leaves with a plastic bag full of salad and beans. I hand his sister the slippers and realise that I don't know her name, only the dog's.

There's no internet in Žiga's flat, so I go to the one other café in town, the one whose name means the white bull: Užitkarna Beli Vol. Žiga told me that there used to be a bar there. He's barely ever at home. He works at an orphanage and the shifts are long, usually 12 hours. When he gets home, his eyes are dull and he doesn't want to talk, but he's happy to drink a few beers while he listens to the Tomažes' made-up stories.

Užitkarna Beli Vol has light wood floors and beautiful modern furniture that isn't so beautiful after all. Close up, the floors and furniture look fake, but I don't know what they're copies of. I usually sit in the imitation leather armchair in the corner because it faces the big window and is next to a socket. I scroll through Facebook, watch the first few episodes of *How I Met Your Mother*, and at four o'clock the woman with four golden retrievers walks past as usual. The dogs walk in single file, and out of the corner of my eye it looks like the same dog walking by over and over again.

I skype you and you show me Hanoi's thunder and

lightning. You show me a massive moth hiding from the rain under the canopy. You're not bored anymore. You've made some new friends who are more exciting than the people you were hanging out with before. The jab in my heart when you say it makes me ask about your job, your colleagues, how the project is going. You don't mention Layla. You don't tell me about how you danced together in a nightclub in Hanoi, the new one with a dance floor on the roof. Layla dances like no one else. If I knew, the jab in my heart would be more than a jab. The pain would spread like fire through my body, and I would burst into flames in the white armchair, leaving soot stains and nothing else behind on the fake leather seat. I'm the one who dances like no one else, who grinds against you and takes you home. You know that, so you don't mention Layla, you just tell me about budding rice fields and humid gravel roads, about the cactus on your desk.

A few weeks later, you go to her place. You drink a glass of wine on the sofa and you probably share a cigarette, and I imagine that her skin is soft, that she doesn't have any ingrown hairs or birthmarks. The kind of skin you want to draw on with a pen. I had no idea you were keeping a secret like that, I say when you tell me about Layla a few months later. It's a lie, but I want to come off cool. Tove Lo sings about being a *cool girl*, and I want to be tough like her. *You can run free, I won't hold it against you.* I won't hold it against you.

I want you to be my model.

I empty the sachet of sugar into my coffee and shake my head, watching the aggression bubbling up inside Tomaž. It settles in droplets above his upper lip. He forgets his pack of cigarettes on the table behind him and I fish out a Marlboro Light as he disappears through the gate, his steps echoing through the courtyard. I buy a train ticket at the station for the next morning, and the cashier behind the glass spins the disc around so I can take my ticket and change. The train will be leaving from Platform 4, he says, looking expectantly at the person in line behind me, and I quickly grab the ticket and coins. The receipt floats down to the concrete floor. It's wet, in the way floors in stations usually are.

I leave in the stillness of the early morning and it's as though I was never here. I pack my bag and sneak down the stairs, out through the front door that slams behind me, giving me away. But it could have been anyone. The postman. The streets are deserted. It's a bank holiday and all the shops are closed. We'll be closed tomorrow, the cashier in the supermarket bakery told me yesterday, just so you know. I nodded and felt the urge to tell this young woman with circles under her eyes that I wasn't coming back. That I wouldn't be buying any more oily cumin bread or croissants. But I didn't say anything because we didn't know each other, and what was she supposed to say? There wasn't anything to say because we had only ever talked about bread and money. Still, I had begun to appreciate our relationship because it was easy to navigate, easy to understand. It was uncomplicated because she was wearing an apron and I wasn't, because she was the cashier and I was the customer. It was a simple relationship, the way she handed me a bag over the counter, gave me five cents in change, carefully folding the receipt in half so it wouldn't be blown away by the ceiling fan, the endlessly rotating blades.

The bear has woken, the time has come, the moon is full, and so on.

Our flat smells different. In my absence it's acquired a sweet, pungent smell, and I walk through the living room, kitchen and bedroom, opening all the windows. The flat relaxes, a door slams and I open it again, putting a chair in front so it doesn't slide shut again. In a sense, the flat is exactly how I left it: the striped shadows of blinds on the floor, the unmade bed, the bowl with leftover milk and oats. That's where the smell is coming from. Mould has spread across the sides of the bowl and up the spoon and I imagine it growing in time with my movements through Škofja Loka, meeting one Tomaž after another. I throw the bowl and the spoon in the bin, collapse on the sofa and feel the sun retreating. Soon the shadows will be painting cool stripes on my face.

Are you home yet?

Are you home yet?

The messages from Mathilde and Simon come one after the

other. The vibration wakes me up. Yes, it's good to be home. I'm just chilling on the sofa, I text Simon. And Mathilde: Yes! Should we do something tonight?

The inside of my rucksack smells like Tomaž. My clothes are wrinkled and stained. I throw them all into the shower, spraying them with water to remove the traces of Marlboro Lights and pumpkin seed dust and cumin. They slide off my clothes and disappear down the drain and I imagine my memories of the Tomažes going down with them.

Mathilde has brought Alexander along with her. They're sitting at a table in the corner, and she's cut her hair. Her temples are even more visible now. The point where her hair meets her forehead seems to move a little every time she opens her mouth. Her eyebrows are pencilled in and her lips are like velvet grazing mine when we give each other a kiss hello. Welcome home, she says, and Alexander gives me a big kiss on the cheek, grabs my hand, gives it a squeeze. It's good to have you back. They don't want to talk about themselves this time, they ask me questions and more questions, laughing and looking at each other. They tell me I look good. We missed you, Mathilde says, and Alexander places a hand on my thigh.

Then the music starts and we have to be quiet. The bartender introduces the house pianist and we clap hesitantly. She plays old Danish love songs and I wish that the golden candlelight were hectic strobe lights instead. I feel the electricity flowing between me and Mathilde. She blows me a kiss and I grab it with a lazy wave of my hand, and the drawn-out love songs, the soft notes on the piano, turn into a heavy techno beat that won't stop. Thumping somewhere out there. I can feel the bass in my cheeks.

It's Alexander's birthday. Mathilde throws a party together and we stock the fridge with Netto champagne, carefully arrange long black cigarettes with gold filters on battered trays of stained silver. I used to fuck a guy who imported cigarettes from Poland, she says. He was terrible in bed, oh my. She tried to end it, but he kept contacting her, texts, calls, showing up on her doorstep unannounced, until finally they reached an agreement. He would hide the black cigarettes with gold filters at Blågårds Plads. One of the granite statues lining the short walls became their designated hiding place. The fisherman's wife bent over her child, displaying a fresh-caught fish, her arms powerful and sinewy. In the space between her bent arm and the head of the fish, the pack of cigarettes lay hidden, almost covered by her granite bonnet. You could only spot them if you knew they were there. Mathilde doesn't need to pay him as long as she lets him know when she'll come to pick them up. He waits in his flat, looking out of his kitchen window. He turns on his camera as soon as she rounds the corner. She

82

could easily just walk down the stairs, stop in front of the statue and pull out the cigarettes, but she doesn't. Instead, she takes her time, pausing behind the fisherman's wife and slowly bending over, and while her hand gropes around the muscular granite, he zooms in and snaps a few pictures from his windowsill.

I ask Mathilde if she isn't bothered by the thought of all those pictures of her taken from the window, her arse when she bends over the statue. She shrugs: We all have our little quirks, don't we?

We find some satin in the discount bin at STOF2000 for twenty kroner a metre, and we stuff bag after bag with the rustling material, and I end up paying because Mathilde's credit card is lying on a dance floor somewhere in Copenhagen. It fell out of her pocket when she was out dancing last night. She can't remember which club, she doesn't know where to look – maybe it was at a bar? They were playing Bowie, now I remember, she says, and tells me that she got everyone at the bar out of their seats, how she spun around one grey alcoholic after another. Round and round until she ran into the bar, that must have been when it fell out, she says. That makes sense.

Back at their flat, we tear the satin apart, draping it over bookshelves and hanging streamers of it from the old chandelier Mathilde inherited from her grandmother. We tape big pieces of satin over the framed posters. We're covering all the frames with satin to make big squares in assorted colours – it'll look like the dance floor at Nightfever! Alexander comes home before the guests arrive, and we scamper around him like kids, showing him one brilliant detail after another.

Look, look, look!

The flat has never looked more beautiful, Alexander says, kissing Mathilde's forehead and then mine, and Simon calls me from Hanoi. I show him the bedroom, the living room, the hallway, moving excitedly from room to room. All right, calm down, he says, I want to take it all in. But I can't calm down, the camera won't focus because I'm moving so frantically, streamers of satin blur into a rainbow on the screen. Mathilde and Alexander are sitting on the balcony and I tell Simon I don't want to disturb them, it's better if he meets them in person. When he comes home.

Mathilde has told everyone to wear white. It'll look so beautiful with all the white and the satin, she says, and finds a patterned silk shirt in her closet with blue accents and a little orange stripe on each sleeve. I look so pale in white, she says, pulling the shirt on over her head. Here, you wear this. She throws me a white lace dress and I let my trousers fall to the ground. Everyone will be able to see my red underwear through the lace, I say. That's not going to work. It looks sexy, she says and zips up the dress for me. Her fingertips brush my bra. And suddenly, the living room is full of dancing people. We're like ecstatic angels with our arms in the air. We can just barely reach the satin streamers dangling from the chandelier, which swings from side to side every time we grab at them. I hope it's a good party, Simon texts me, and I write a few words and then Mathilde is there – she grabs my phone and puts it in her pocket and we dance close together in the middle of all the people in white. Her hands on my hips, a little squeeze.

The dance floor closes when the sun rises and everyone's white clothes are stained with beer and ash. But the party isn't over, not yet. Mathilde leads everyone to their big bed. She sits in the middle, enthroned like a kingfisher in a nest of cotton. The ashtray is passed around, a last bottle of bubbles rolls out – it was hiding under the bed – and someone shirtless shakes it and the mattress shakes too, my breasts bouncing softly up and down. POP! The cork hits the ceiling. Mathilde gets the bottle first, she tips her head back and holds the bottle with both hands. Some goes down the wrong pipe and bubbling snot comes out of her nose. She's still the most beautiful one here.

Simon sends me his flight number and arrival time, and I check whether his flight is delayed. I check again. His flight is still *on time* according to the app on my phone. I stand in the shower and turn up the hot water, turning the tap until it won't turn anymore. The water can't be hot enough today. After the shower it's like my body won't dry, my skin is still wet and warm, and as I stick a foot into my tights my thigh cramps and I have to massage it to get my foot all the way in, and my little toe chafes against the thin nylon material. My toenail is almost popping through. I want to text Simon that I have a cramp, that I can't get my shoes on, that I can't pick him up from the airport, but I don't because I know he can't answer. He's sitting on an aircraft letting himself be carried through the clouds, and as I wobble down to the bus stop, I imagine him watching my limping walk through the little window above. Breathing on the glass and drawing a heart with his finger.

Families with Danish flags and boyfriends and girl-friends with roses are clustered together in the arrival hall, and I realise that I should have bought something for Simon, that I'm the only one standing here empty-handed. He'll probably look the same, right? one of the girlfriends says to her mother-in-law. The mother-in-law gives her shoulder a gentle squeeze. The girlfriend is trembling with expectant joy, she can't stand still, she shifts her weight from one foot to the other. The cellophane around the roses crackles.

I can't wait to see you, Simon texts me. The screen fills with hearts, it's like they're trying to push themselves out of the screen. I put my phone back in my pocket and look determinedly at the screen with arrival times. My perfume makes my eyes water and I can feel my contact lenses sticking every time I blink. The left one gets caught under my eyelid and it stings when I push it back into place with my index finger. I can blame my red eyes on my dry contact lenses, I think, searching for my lip balm in my pocket, smearing a little extra in the corners of my mouth. Mathilde hasn't just left red lines in my eyes, she's taken the moisture from my lips too; maybe she's trying to sabotage our reunion kiss.

And then he's standing in front of me, sunburned and too blond, and he kisses me. His stubble prickles against my dry upper lip. Welcome home, I say, taking one of his bags, and he kisses my head and puts an arm around my waist. We walk like that through the airport among all the other reunited couples.

Everything is packed and ready. My things are in the moving boxes in the living room and Simon's have been in the attic since he left for Hanoi. Spiderwebs cover his boxes like sticky threads and dusty light falls through the skylight. Toke comes over at noon to help in his worn-out joggers. I can't wait to live with you guys, he says. We say cheers with our cokes, and Dina arrives, standing on the stairs in colourful trainers and shorts that are a little too short, ready to carry our big boxes, and I don't understand why she's offering to help because usually she's very lazy.

Dina gives Toke's back a little smack as he edges past her in the cramped storage space. The dimples in her cheeks are deep and dark. She tries to pick up a box and it slips out of her hands. Toke, she says laughing, I need your help, and the way she says it makes me want to tell her that we don't need their help after all. Get out of here! I want to scream, but I don't because there are a lot of boxes to move. We're not strong enough to carry them by ourselves.

We lug boxes of books and cutlery and clothes down the

stairs. The rug from the charity shop down the street. Toke and Simon make fun of each other's wheezing and sweaty foreheads. They high five every time they pass each other in the stairwell.

Your new place is amazing, Dina says, you won't ever have to move again. We're all standing in the large kitchen in the old flat and I don't know how to respond. She hands me our hand blender and says: I think there's still some room in the last box. I put the blender in the box and lay my denim jacket on top of it. Dina grabs our PH lamp and disappears down the stairs. I stand there for a moment, looking around the empty flat. It suddenly feels impossible to leave these rooms behind. Are you ready, Simon asks, handing me the last moving box. He leans over to give me a kiss. Prickling my upper lip.

We can't wait to meet him, Mathilde texts me, and they join us at Café Intime. Simon buys a round of beers and does most of the talking. He tells them about Hanoi and the city's burgeoning club scene, about the poor farmers who are finally being compensated for their land, the land that was taken away from them by big multinational corporations. The pride on the bridge of his nose. His nose seems straighter than it was before he left. We changed their lives! he says. Mathilde and Alexander follow Simon's movements with their eyes, watching him roll up the sleeves of his floral shirt, raise the bottle to his mouth, and I hear myself say: In this bar, we use glasses.

Mathilde and Alexander have an open marriage, I say. They're allowed to sleep with other people. Simon pours his beer into a glass, looks up. It's like he's seeing them for the first time, feeling their gaze on his body. How does that work, he asks, and Mathilde and Alexander take the stage: they're a two-man band ready to wow the audience with the elaborate show they've been practising for years.

Simon's face changes colour in time with the light from the cars driving past outside, their headlights streaming through the stained-glass windows, turning green, orange and dark red, and Mathilde hits the final note: We want to change the world, we're setting love free! Simon laughs and says cheers. His cheeks are red and his tan looks more like a burn, and he buys four shots of Fernet Branca at the bar, almost tripping over himself in his eagerness to hand them out to us. He says cheers again and gives me a wet kiss on the cheek. I've been thinking the same thing, he says, winking at me, our love wouldn't be threatened by us sleeping with other people, would it? He looks me in the eyes, and even though my eyes are focused on him, I can feel Mathilde's indulgent smile. That has to be the right way to do it, he says, that must be true love. It's so obvious, you can tell just by looking at Mathilde and Alexander, he says, throwing his hands out as if the whole bar should be looking at them, but no one notices, everyone is already occupied by something else.

All of a sudden, Mathilde wants to go home. She stands up and gives me a kiss goodbye, gives Simon a big hug across the table, and Alexander puts his jacket on, then holds Mathilde's jacket up behind her so she can put her arms through its sleeves. They disappear to the sound of the bartender calling last round. Simon buys two beers, and he seems agitated. I bite my lip and he bites his, mirroring me. I slept with someone else, he says. And the stained-glass windows, the walls, the ceiling disappear, and I can see the clouds

91

above us moving slowly across the sky heavy with rain. But there aren't any clouds, only a pair of heels tied to the ceiling with thin laces, lazily dangling in the smoke. Simon tells me about Layla, about the way she danced, her breasts bouncing from side to side, about how he felt the urge to hold them in place with his hands. And then I did, he says, and his voice is a whisper. Maybe he's hoping that I can't hear what he's saying. He tells me about the night on the sofa, how his dick ended up in her vagina. I only started to feel guilty afterwards, he says. The lights are turned on and the music off, and only a few foreign voices remain, other people laughing boisterously, and I don't say anything. I don't know what to say.

Are you okay?

The duvet smells new like IKEA and we crawl under it. Simon squeezes my nipple and I think about how there's no way that Layla's nipples are as big as mine, they're probably beautiful and pointy all the time, always ready to be squeezed between two fingers. Mine need to be squeezed hard before they get pointy, and they soften again right away, my chest is like a man's. Flat, brown nipples, nothing to fill your hand. I'm totally fine, I say, and Simon nuzzles the other nipple, trying to make it hard, and I repeat: I'm fine, it's fine. He runs his fingers through my hair, and we lie close together, me with my soft nipples and Simon with his head somewhere else.

Should we give it a try?

What do you mean, I say, and Simon laughs and kisses me at the same time so his laugh is transferred to my mouth. For my sake, it's fine if you want to have sex with other people, he says, breaking off the kiss. I don't want to have sex with other people for your sake, I should say, but instead I smile and push his boxer shorts down with my big toe. The rain is beating against the window. His orgasm is silent, but his eyelids move a little.

Alexander doesn't look like himself, the MDMA has drawn his face in new directions and his features have disappeared. He yanks open the door to the bar, raising his hands over his head, and he swings his jacket around like it's a cape and he's Sirius Black. He howls in my ear, pulls me out of my chair and spins me around: I want to fuck you right here! he says over and over again. I kiss him greedily, there isn't anything else to do.

I texted Mathilde earlier, but she didn't reply, and I found a red lipstick in the bottom of my bag and took the bus to Det Rene Glas, sat down at the table closest to the door. I started a little every time it opened or closed. I tried to sit with my back to the door, but it didn't help, her face was everywhere. She was sitting on the bench in the back, fishing a cigarette out of a crumpled pack, or at the bar drinking shots with one of the regulars. In the bathroom, a woman in line had Mathilde's chin. She snapped at me to look where I was going when I bumped into her, and I gave up, found Mathilde's number on my phone. The voice on her answerphone was automatic and heartbreaking, I couldn't listen to the whole thing. Are you with Mathilde, I texted Alexander, I'm at Det Rene Glas. He responded with three sparkling blue diamonds, and suddenly he was there – without her.

The high dissipates from his body, or he's transferred his high to me through our kiss. Now I'm the unstoppable one. I can't stop touching and licking Alexander and I text Simon that I won't be coming home tonight. Where are you sleeping? he answers immediately, and I write that I'm staying at Mathilde and Alexander's. His silence is sufficient, there's no going back now. Alexander finds his bicycle fallen over on the pavement, we cycle through the night, and I feel it throbbing between my legs, maybe I'm horny, or maybe it's because the pannier rack is pressing against my clitoris.

Your hair smells like coffee, Alexander says sliding his fingers through a handful of hair, trying to untangle the knots. Can I cut it off? My head is resting in the right curve of his pelvis, his slack penis feels soft against my ear. You look like you're about to eat my hair, Mathilde does the same thing, I laugh, and he takes another chunk of hair between his index and middle finger, spreading it apart and gathering it back together as if his fingers were a pair of scissors. I can feel his dick against my cheek, but I don't move my head. I say: You can't cut my hair.

What do you need all this hair for?

I don't have the chance to answer. Suddenly, she's standing right there in front of the bed. She's still wearing her coat, with a thin scarf tied tightly around her neck. The cigarette in her hand has burned down to the filter, but it's still glowing between her fingers. Alexander pushed the ashtray under the bed last night, he kept tripping over it.

Good morning.

She takes a drag, but no smoke goes into her lungs, there's no more tobacco left, and she throws the butt into a half-empty wine glass. We should get to the office, Alice. My clothes are spread across the floor, and I pull the duvet around me, finding my trousers first and then my leotard.

She lingers in the doorway and gives Alexander a kiss goodbye and I hurry down the stairs, unable to make myself wait for her.

Another weekend. Simon has a headache. He takes the duvet to the sofa with him and makes room for me, but everything in the flat is telling me to leave. The windows howl and the rug bunches together beneath my feet. You're buzzing today, Simon says, and I don't know whether he's intrigued or repulsed. I stumble getting off the sofa. The white walls make me hyperventilate, Simon's gaze pierces my back, I need to get out of here – now. Anywhere is better than home right now, and yet home is the only place I want to be. I give Simon a kiss goodbye. He doesn't look me in the eyes. His lips are a straight line across his face, they feel dry against mine.

You look nice, Dina says, and she buys a bottle of wine. We're handed a bucket of ice and a glass filled to the brim with peanuts. We sit outside in the heated section with the bucket on the table between us, listening to the ice cubes melting and feeling rich, beautiful. All the men are looking at you, Dina says, but I don't notice any flirtatious glances, I can't focus. Dina's face is suddenly runny: lipstick, foundation and a thick layer of mascara slide off her face, and when I blink again, the face of a clown is smiling grotesquely back at me. I escape to the bathroom, making sure the door is locked. Finally a message from Mathilde. Are you coming? she writes, and Dina looks disappointed when I pour the last of the wine into her glass and tell her that I have to run. The clown face is gone when I look back and wave, Dina's make-up is back in place again. She pretends not to notice my wave.

Bar laughter and loud outbursts of joy, bottlenecks clinking against each other, Mathilde's gesticulations and white teeth, drinks extraordinarily served at the table by the bartender, Alexander's hand on my thigh. Everything all over again. Mathilde has her eyes on a guy at the bar, he's the one she'll go home with tonight. She's made up her mind, and acid rises in my throat when she points him out, nodding in his direction, her earrings glittering. Isn't he hot?

I'm not coming home tonight, I text Simon, and he answers: I expected as much. Are you angry? I type it but don't press send because I can't deal with his answer, not right now when Mathilde is raising her glass and kissing my earlobe. I love you, she slurs, and her breath is warm and wet, and for a second, I think she means it.

Alexander draws the curtains forcefully; the curtain rod bends a little in the middle and straightens again. I find my phone on the bedside table, see the messages from Simon, reading them with blurry hungover eyes. He has a bad feeling, it's too soon for this to be happening again. Early in the morning, he sent a last message: Come home. And I imagine Simon walking restlessly around the flat at night, the rug smooth and soft under the soles of his feet. Maybe he went out on the balcony to smoke a cigarette, to watch the sunrise alone. I almost can't bear the thought.

Where are you going?

Alexander takes my hands and holds them tight above my head and my phone falls to the floor. You can't leave, he murmurs, and it feels like this morning will never end. You can't make me stay just so Mathilde will see us, I want to say, but I wait with him. He gets his way, if it's even his way – maybe it's mine. We flip through the newspaper in bed without reading, my phone makes a little sound to let me know it's dying. And then we fuck. Alexander keeps looking towards the door, finishing himself off on my chest like a dog marking his territory. It's too much, it's too late, and I'm supposed to go with Simon to his friend's house for brunch. I grab some tissues to clean myself up, borrow a T-shirt from Alexander. It smells like Mathilde.

Simon is waiting for me in front of the bakery. He doesn't want to talk about it right now. He doesn't want to be late.

My reflection isn't mine. My face has changed, I think as I line my tired eyes with black eyeliner. My face is haggard, my cheeks droop like used tea bags. But I have to go.

Mathilde answers the door in her underwear and a T-shirt. Her underwear is crispy white and her slender thighs don't touch each other when she walks through the living room in front of me. Gold glitter trainers and tennis socks. My heart is in my throat, no, higher than that, it's like my brain and my heart are glued together. I'm about to be broken up with. I'm about to lose her, I know it and I feel it. But then it doesn't happen because Mathilde is fumbling for words – she's nervous – which makes me feel surer of myself. My brain and heart slide apart again. Are her hands shaking more than usual?

I still don't understand what happened on Friday, my memory is full of holes, foggy and fragmented. Still, the night lingers in my diaphragm, stinging my lungs. It's been two days since Friday, since everything started to fall apart. I never see her on Sundays. Sunday is our day of rest, but today I'm here, because of Friday.

What happened on Friday?

The question flaps around the room, but neither of us dares to grab it. Mathilde brings two wine glasses from the kitchen. They clink when she puts them down and only then does she notice the silence. She turns on the radio and I want to ask her to turn it off, there's no room for music here. But I don't say anything. We just listen to the radio in silence. Why doesn't she ask me:

What happened on Friday?

It started at the bar on Stefansgade. My friends had started drinking early. Their eyes were shrunken with alcohol as they shouted over each other. It was difficult to concentrate. I watched mouth after mouth opening, but I couldn't hear the sounds coming out. Their words dissolved in the haze of smoke. I was bored by their company, all the flannel shirts and canvas shoes. I took a cab to Mathilde and Alexander's. They were having some friends over and Mathilde was sitting at the end of the table smoking a thin cigarette: the queen was holding court. And then the fool arrived with her cap and bells on, her upturned shoes. I left my jacket in the hallway, kept my shoes on.

Did I call you?

Mathilde looked away as she asked, crossing her legs and rocking a bit back and forth on her chair. There weren't enough chairs at the table. I leaned against the windowsill instead, feeling the peeling paint ripping runs in my tights. Alexander texted me, I said. And that was the first time I saw it, that sour expression. Mathilde bared her cuspids and laughed, made a sarcastic comment, and her minions laughed too. Alexander didn't get a beer for me. I had to find one in the fridge. Everything whirled when I closed it, the flat with its battered and nicotine-yellow walls was like a drug in itself. And then Mathilde touched Alexander's arm and a golden glow was cast over him: everything she touches turns to gold. There's no king of this kingdom, the queen rules alone, and now she wants to go out. I'm feeling claustrophobic, she says, and the courtiers push their chairs away from the table and rise, grab their coats, bend down to tie their shoelaces. Let's go! Mathilde is ready to leave. Turn off the lights, she orders. The cab is here, Alexander says, and we run down the stairs. We squeeze together in the backseat as the others disappear on bicycles in front of us. A scarf falls out of a basket, but the lady-in-waiting doesn't dare stop to pick it up. The queen wants to go to a party, and when the queen wants to go to a party, there's no time to waste.

Have you met Alice?

Mathilde introduces me over and over, and embarrassed, I say hello and make small talk, say thank you for the drink. The speakers are broken, but we're trying to keep it going, the host of the party says.

The speakers are fixed and the music comes back on, but the dance floor is lethargic and we move lazily to the music. It's as if the bass doesn't want to enter our bodies, it's everywhere except inside us. They disappear, Mathilde and Alexander, and I'm suddenly alone in a sea of faceless dancers. Excuse me, I say pushing past a shoulder, squeezing through a wall of backs. A stray hand hits my cheek and no one apologises.

There you are.

Her leg on his lap, his hands in her hair, entwined on the sofa like conjoined twins, and there isn't any room for me. But I sit down on the armrest, feel my arm reaching around Alexander's neck and forcing his lips towards mine.

I'm too drunk to kiss you.

And I light a cigarette and ash falls on the sofa. I throw my feet up on the coffee table and a bottle of beer tips over, spreading into a dark stain on the rug, and Alexander kisses Mathilde. She cups her hands around his neck, tightly holding it between her palms as if she's trying to guard it from my gaze. His neck is hers too. We would really like to talk, just the two of us, she says with lips swollen from kissing, and Alexander leans back on the sofa, his back pushes me over the armrest. I have to put my foot on the floor and tense my thigh to avoid falling onto the floor. I can't breathe. The conjoined twins have used up all the oxygen and I stagger to the bathroom, startled by my own reflection, by the junkie staring back at me.

The sofa was unoccupied when I came back from the bathroom, the imprint of their backsides barely visible in the circles of light from the disco ball. I remember running down the stairs, stumbling and slipping down a few steps and getting back up again, yanking the door to the building open just in time – in time to see them disappear, two black coats swallowed by the inside of a cab.

We don't mention that either this Sunday. We talk about work, our unimportant jobs, and Mathilde rolls one joint and then another. Sia's voice on the radio. The speaker is small and the song sounds like a distant echo of Friday night.

Well I've got thick skin and an elastic heart, but your blade it might be too sharp.

We act like nothing happened. We lazily pass the joint back and forth. We take turns holding smoke in our lungs and slowly breathing out. You can stay the night if you want, Mathilde says and puts out the joint, turning off the radio.

Alexander comes home at two in the morning. I watch him from the bed. He's standing in front of the computer in its pale light. Was he making noise on purpose?

He carefully places the condom on the bedside table so the semen won't run out. There's a little blood on the condom – my period wasn't over after all – and Mathilde makes a noise like she's sleeping and I don't want to believe that she's awake. We won't talk about this night either, yet another night we won't talk about, and Alexander sleeps restlessly between us. I get up and smoke a cigarette, feeling that this is the last time I'll be in their bedroom. I feel them watching me for the last time from their bed. Two sets of closed eyes that can endure anything, believe everything.

Dina says I'm in over my head, she says I'm obsessed like she's never seen before, she's worried about me. What they're doing to me. She thinks I need to stop, and I say that I want to, but it's difficult. I think about Morten's warning. Morten's body on the pavement, a pile of shattered bones and clothes torn to pieces. Simon finding my body wrecked in the same way. Simon sulking, powerless, unable to comprehend how it got to this point.

I watch Dina and Toke drinking their coffee in the kitchen and I dream about being satisfied by that kind of relationship, by tooth-brushing and spooning. Their way of being together is touching, it's not tainted by entangled tongues. Their relationship is pure and calm. They'll chew you up, Morten said, and I'm letting myself be devoured bit by bit, but it's not like I'm holding back. I satiate my own hunger too. Three cannibals frothing at the mouth with bloodshot eyes. We peel the meat off each other's bones. We slurp and crunch and swallow and belch.

Simon is watching me from the living room. Without turning around I can feel him leaning against the doorframe with his hand in his pocket. He's either calm or afraid. I can't tell the difference anymore.

She's tightly wound.

Toke squashes his cigarette on the wall under the window. There are black marks on the bricks from all the cigarettes he's stubbed out. You can see them from the street, like day-old eyeliner, fiery black streaks of soot on the wall. Toke flicks the butt of his cigarette to the pavement and says: There's nothing to figure out, she's an ice queen. And I think that Mathilde is tightly wound, taut like a sheet stretched over a mattress that I want to throw myself onto. I want to feel the tight whiteness against my spine, my buttocks. To feel the smooth fabric. I have to lie entirely still to avoid sliding over the edge and onto the floor.

Have you forgotten about Simon?

It's an accusation in the shape of a question, and because he asks that way, it also becomes the answer: I've forgotten about Simon. He's disappeared in my dreams about the sheet. But he also hasn't because I'm not letting myself go all the way. I'm a coward living in my own fantasies, hiding in Alexander's embrace. His moans are horny, mine are hesitant.

Of course I haven't!

Of course you have?

Toke misunderstands me on purpose. He wants a confession, but he doesn't get one. Deny, deny, deny, Peter shouts in Paradise Hotel, and I'm the denying fuckboi, but I'm not in paradise. I just am. Here and there, but mostly there: in daydreams about Mathilde's thigh on my cheek, her clitoris on the tip of my tongue. I think about Laura's flapping plaits as she flew down the asphalt ramp, how I followed her without hesitation. I long for my childhood courage. Was my cunt already sprouting at the age of 12? I think so, but I don't remember it as a process. My sex appeared between my legs overnight, with all of its significations in tow. Maybe it sprouted from my courage, maybe my courage turned into my cunt, courage was used to build my lips and clitoris, and that's why I have a cunt now but no courage. What am I supposed to use my cunt for if I don't dare do more than dream?

Simon tells me that I'm acting a bit off, that I've been acting off ever since Alexander and I started fucking each other. That's how he says it: fucking each other. We don't talk about breaking up, we've agreed not to. We don't talk about how maybe we never really worked together. I tell Dina that Simon thinks I'm different when I'm with my friends. Dina asks if maybe I'm just different around Simon? I know I'm different with Mathilde, I want to say, I'm different when we're walking through Nørrebro and she rests her head on my shoulder, her arm around my waist. After a few steps, she withdraws her head and the slight pressure on my shoulder disappears, but her arm remains, resting on my hip. The pavement narrows as we near Queen Louise's Bridge. Bicycles are parked in front of all the bars, shopping bags are lugged past us. The plastic grazes my leg and Mathilde pulls me closer, as though to protect me from all the stuffed plastic bags and bicycle wheels. The pavement is ours, suddenly nothing can touch me, no one but her. Let's buy a bottle of wine, she says, and we go into Fakta. We find the cheapest wine with a screw cap and wait in the queue. The cold LED lights and sticky linoleum floor and the sound of the scanner beeping. Everything is different with her.

One night, Alexander is delightfully mine. He carries me through the living room and the hallway, past the bathroom and the kitchen, and he puts me down where Mathilde's head has left a permanent dent in the pillow over the years, a dent now filled by me. And I imagine Mathilde and I are one, Alexander having sex with us fused together, and it doesn't matter which of us is in bed with him because I am Mathilde and Mathilde is me, we're the same. Can you love your own mirror image? I'm Narcissus: I can only love my reflection. It's the only form of love I know.

But just like Narcissus needs the surface of the water between himself and the depths, I need Alexander. I touch Alexander's body where Mathilde's hands have touched, I grab his dick and imagine Mathilde's fingers around it. Mathilde's fingers unbuttoning her winter coat, Mathilde's fingers stubbing out another cigarette, Mathilde's fingers around my neck. Mathilde's fingers on my clitoris, the way they're moving right now, ah! Mathilde's hands on my hips. She grabs my phone on the dance floor, she kisses me, her tongue is lazy in my mouth. I don't dare say: You're the one I want to be with, you're the one I want. The pathetic satisfaction of letting my head sink into her pillow, envisioning the imprint of her head against the back of mine. I see women in the changing rooms at the swimming pool. I see perfect breasts and pretty cunts and soft earlobes, but those women's bodies are unimportant, it's not about them. It's about Mathilde.

But it's also about more than her.

Alexander is between my legs, his tongue on my clitoris, and I wish I could tell him why he's lying there. It has nothing to do with his body. I don't care about men's bodies or women's bodies when I think about Mathilde. But it still means something, there's still a reason I'm in bed with him and not her. As I feel his breath on my cunt, I imagine a world where a body is a body and a human is a human.

A kiss – a kiss.

It's the anniversary of the demolition of Ungdomshuset. Firecrackers thunder in the distance and soon they'll be exploding right outside our door. The windows rattle from the reverberations, masked people dressed in black are throwing cobblestones, shop windows shatter. It feels like the windows of our flat are about to splinter into a thousand pieces. Neither you nor Toke are wearing masks and I think about the new law that says you can be arrested just for being in the proximity of someone smashing windows or setting off firecrackers during a protest. That's how our dodgy system functions: politicians and government officials don't actually care about masked people vandalising property. People like you and Toke are the ones they're afraid of. What are we going to do if the majority rallies together to overthrow the system? politicians and government officials probably whispered among themselves. So they found a solution and made it a law: it won't only be people in masks getting arrested, but all the dangerous peaceful protesters too.

There's nothing revolutionary about daily life in our

building. The flagpole is the surveillance tower of our panoptic prison, cameras are attached to the top. They're watching us and we're not supposed to take a stand on anything. The washing machine has an automatic detergent dispenser and the landlord mows the lawn even though the dandelions are blooming yellow. We don't greet our neighbours in the stairwell. We drive the time away with our daily routines.

Toke and Simon discussed the unlawful use of force and revolution as they prepared for the protest. Today we're taking a stand, they said, and then they ran down the stairs. I'm not taking a stand. I scroll through news updates on Local Eyes and Ekstra Bladet because they cover protests more than other newspapers, and I wish that I didn't care, that I could just sit on the windowsill with my mint tea and pretend that the explosions in the distance were thunder. The fires on my computer screen ignite something inside me, and I call you, call you, call you. Your voice:

You've called Simon. I can't answer the phone right now, please ring back later.

His words are slow and slightly slurred. I was drunk when I recorded it and I don't want to record a new one, you once said. Tonight your slurred voice on the answerphone provokes me. You need to answer, you need to come home. The fight is here, not in the streets, and it has to be today. Come home, I order in my voice message. I hang up and call again. Suddenly, you're standing in the hallway, and the windows are rattling even more than before. The whole flat is shaking and I'm not crying. I say:

Why should I be punished for sleeping with someone else, when you're not?

You say that it doesn't have anything to do with sleeping with other people. It's about how I'm behaving. Nothing I do is good enough for you, I say. You're always trying to change me – adjusting the volume, the bass. The entire song is different by the time you're done.

WHY DO I ALWAYS HAVE TO BE THE ONE WHO'S NOT GOOD ENOUGH. WHY DO I ALWAYS HAVE TO BE THE ONE WHO NEEDS TO GET MY SHIT TOGETHER. YOU DON'T HAVE YOUR FUCKING SHIT TOGETHER. WE AGREED IT WAS OKAY AS LONG AS WE WERE HONEST WITH EACH OTHER. I LIE BUT IT'S ONLY BECAUSE YOU'RE LYING TOO. YOU LIED FIRST. I'M JUST FOL-LOWING YOUR EXAMPLE. WHAT ELSE AM I SUPPOSED TO DO. JUST LEAVE ME ALREADY, THERE'S ALREADY SO MUCH YOU DON'T LIKE ABOUT ME. THAT'S YOUR EXCUSE. YOU CAN LEAVE ME BECAUSE I SLEPT WITH SOMEONE ELSE. MATHILDE'S HUSBAND. SOMEONE ELSE'S DICK HAS BEEN INSIDE ME AND THAT'S TOO MUCH FOR YOU TO DEAL WITH. FINE.

It wasn't really a decision. I didn't google the words menstrual cup or IUD. I didn't call my doctor or gynaecologist. Maybe it had something to do with Alexander's insistence on using condoms or the way Simon was always rolling onto his side whenever I reached for his dick. Or maybe my head was somewhere else when I realised that my IUD was stuck to my menstrual cup and I just pulled anyway. Maybe I was thinking about Mathilde. I pulled the medical-grade silicone all the way out and time and space dissolved. The only thing left was the movement of pulling. The white tiles in the bathroom disappeared and my whole consciousness sank into my vagina and closed off all sensation in the rest of my body. My fingers belonged to someone else when they reached towards my cervix, searching for the spot where my menstrual cup and IUD were stuck together, and it was like the plastic arms of the IUD were tearing and flaying someone else's vagina.

I sat there on the toilet with my tights around my ankles and the menstrual cup and IUD in my hands. I could feel the sweat between my breasts, my ears were ringing and my abdomen was hurting in a different way to when the gynaecologist inserted the IUD. You don't need to watch, the gynaecologist said when I sat down in the black, shell-shaped chair in the clinic. The gynaecologist picked up the box and threw the bag and receipt into the steel bin: Take off your trousers and underwear and put them on the chair.

A poster from the zoo was mounted on the ceiling. Look at the poster and open your legs, the gynaecologist said, can you move down a little? I focused on a giraffe with big cartoon eyes while the gynaecologist fumbled with the box, the sound of a thin plastic bag being torn open. The elephant was spraying water out of its trunk and the gynaecologist told me I could press down on my stomach with both hands. It's a little trick I invented for it not to hurt. Can you give me a big cough? I coughed and gasped and squeezed my eyes closed as the gynaecologist drove a foreign body into my uterus, something that wasn't at home in a body of muscles and bones and secretions. The gynaecologist asked me to put my trousers back on and leave the room and I grabbed my trousers and underwear from the chair, put on my coat and waddled down to the street where I sat down on a bench and cried a little as I thought about all the sex I was going to have. All the pointless, pleasurable sex, culminating each time with sperm cells attempting in vain to break through the hormonal barrier inside my cervix.

I read online that my IUD contains progestogen, that it's a very reliable method of birth control. The IUD will make the mucous membranes of my uterus a less hospitable environment for a fertilised egg and cause changes in the secretions of my cervix to obstruct the movement of sperm cells. It's ideal for young women who haven't given birth, I read, and women often experience fewer and less painful periods. All side-effects the sexually active woman can benefit from. And I feel the folds swelling between my legs, how his hands pull them apart. It doesn't matter who he is. All hands feel the same in that moment.

I love period cramps. The nagging feeling of something being released – of the body at work. I also hate them, period cramps, but mostly because I don't want to admit that I'm a little absent today, that my body is out of sorts because thick red slime is oozing out of me.

Let me bleed in peace.

I didn't have fewer periods, but the pain went from being wide and heavy to sharp and stabbing, as if it had found a new epicenter: the miniature plastic uterus. I think I can feel it, Simon complained when inside me, and I said that there wasn't anything I could do about it. There also isn't anything I can do about cramps or irregular periods, the gynaecologist told me. That's just the price you pay. There's always a price to pay, isn't there?

I took my time observing it in the bathroom, turning the rod with its two plastic arms between my fingers, pulling the small thread and closing my hand around it. It was soft and organic to the touch. I felt my own warmth inside its white plastic, two years of warmth inside something I had never seen before, which I wasn't allowed to see when the gynaecologist put the forceps in place and told me to cough. That's just the price you pay. You're not allowed to see your IUD before it becomes a part of you, you're not allowed to know your progestogen levels or the risk of pregnancy outside your uterus. You can't do anything about the side effects and that's just the way it is. It's a dangerous world if you have a uterus, and you have to protect yourself with hormone-filled pieces of plastic inside you. The alternative is worse, the alternative of hormones rushing through your body that give you acne and sore breasts and quadruple your risk of blood clots. The very worst alternative remains un-named. No one says the word condom. Condom is a curse word at the gynaecologist, in sex-education classes, in conversations with friends. Men don't like condoms, they ruin the experience. They make their orgasms rubbery and weak. And condoms are so difficult to put on correctly. This is how you do it, the nurse said in our sex-education class as she fixed the condom around the penis dummy. But I didn't get a condom. I didn't get a dummy to practice on. It wasn't necessary because condoms are party killers. They should be avoided at all costs. An IUD is a party starter, and you can't go to a party without having a hangover the next day. Maybe you throw up because you drank too many beers. That's life.

The IUD is clean and white except for a bit of reddish slime on one of its arms and I wash it in the sink, dry it off with some toilet paper. There aren't any pockets in my dress or my shirt. Slowly, I untie the laces of my boot and push it in. The little plastic uterus suspended between my shoe and my ankle. My menstrual cup is sitting on the sink, I put it back in, wash my hands and open the door to a contraception-free day. I remember the contraceptive pills, how I was always forgetting to take them. I remember the violent migraines and my doctor's wide eyes when I told her that I was having them. I remember her asking, offended: Why didn't you say something? And I remember changing to a new generation of pills with their neat pink packaging. I remember the miniature pills in the health-food-green box. I remember how they never really worked, how there were constantly issues and pregnancy tests in the bathroom cabinet. I thought you had it under control, Simon would say when I didn't get my period, and I'd say that I thought I did too. I felt the cold sweat breaking out on my forehead as I tried to hit the little piece of plastic with my urine again. Waiting a few minutes, unsure of exactly how many lines indicate life.

The IUD fits better in my boot than where it was before. With every step, it slides further down until finally it's under the ball of my foot, pressing gently into it. Maybe it's missing my warm cervix. Maybe I'm missing its cool piercing pain.

Sunday haunts me. Mathilde didn't hold the buzzer down long enough for me to open the door, so I press the button again. I can feel her irritation seeping down the stairs, making the soles of my shoes sticky, and I have to raise my knees up to my stomach to unstick them from each and every step. I untangle my headphones from my plait as she gives me a hug. Maybe she thought I wasn't coming over until later. She's wearing large white knickers, a dingy white T-shirt.

I just texted Alexander to ask him which wine we can drink, she says. Once I drank one of the expensive ones and he wasn't too happy. The flat is boiling and I take off my T-shirt. I'm wearing my new velvet bra and it seems at home in this flat. The black material contrasts with all her faded whites. She's wearing her gold trainers. Why are you wearing your shoes inside, I want to ask, why are you wearing those shoes? She knows I love her gold shoes and it can't be a coincidence that their soles are now resting in the middle of the dining table, the skin on her thighs bulging a bit on the edge of the table. You didn't like me on Friday, I say.

I always like you, but there are degrees, you know?

You just left without saying goodbye, I confront her. We thought you already left, she says, stealing another one of my cigarettes. She blows the smoke into the air, it floats like a thin orange cloud under the lamp. There are many safe zones in our game of tag and we light more cigarettes and open another bottle of wine, this one looks expensive. We hop from safe zone to safe zone: work, her summer holiday plans, work, what we did yesterday, work again. Work is our most important safe zone, and our game is slow and lazy, as if neither of us really care enough to chase or run away. Our conversation is timid and our roles aren't clearly defined, or they're so well-defined that we don't even notice them anymore.

You can stay the night if you want, she says and stubs out the joint. We hold each other. I'm only in my underwear and her body is small and soft. She's still wearing her T-shirt. I didn't see her untie the gold shoes, but her feet are bare under the duvet, entangled in mine. Sleep well, sweetie, she says and gives me a kiss on the forehead, a kiss that makes the walls shake and the moon sigh. It's probably the last time I'll be in this bed, and I want to cry and laugh. My smile can catch my tears.

Suddenly, Alexander is standing at the end of the table with his eyes fixed on his computer. The embers of his cigarette are violet in the light from the screen and I see that his shirt is too big for his skinny body. His oversized trousers are loose around the hips. My arms are still asleep as they curl around his shoulders, my hands pull his head back and he makes the same sound he always makes before kissing me, the sound of having lost, the sound of submission. I ask: What are you listening to? What are you watching? He doesn't respond, absentmindedly caresses my thigh, and I repeat: You woke me up, what are you watching? I can put on some music for you, he says and pulls up a song on YouTube that I forget as soon as it's over, but I remember the pastel album cover. I remember that and his blazer hanging on the chair. I put it on and my nipples soften in its warmth. I don't understand why he and Mathilde are together, but that's just how it's supposed to be. My toes, my calves, my thighs are frozen, my belly and my breasts are sweating. He hands me the rest of his cigarette:

Should we go to bed?

If this were a film, this sex scene would be accompanied by a song by The Weeknd, most likely *High for This,* and the director would receive glowing reviews for their use of such an untraditional soundtrack. The screen would be a little too blue to suggest melancholy, a classic technique. Here, there's no background music or colour grading, only the sound of Mathilde pretending to sleep – she's not asleep, I realise – and Alexander's moans. I close my eyes and wish that he were different, that we were different, that I weren't just hearing Mathilde's heavy breathing but could feel her exhale on my throat. If only her whimpers weren't tense, if only they were passionate. It's beautiful, Mathilde said that day on the bench. There's nothing beautiful about it.

That wasn't what we agreed, was it?

Simon is the one asking, but it could easily be me, even if it couldn't. I wouldn't have asked. I would have said: It's not what we agreed, but... It's difficult to answer his question because I know that it wasn't what we agreed, but it's happening nevertheless, the loss of control. Simon is trying to take control by making my loss of it his own. He disappears one weekend without telling me where to and I don't try ringing him. I know his phone is off. The bartender at Det Rene Glas asks me where he is, her favourite regulars haven't broken up, have they? And I shake my head smiling, order a beer. Simon returns Sunday night. My phone died, he says, and he doesn't say anything else. His forehead is cold and clammy. His shirt smells like smoke and dance floor.

I want to tell him that I'm in love with Mathilde when we're sitting on the windowsill, his hand resting on my thigh. His fingers move a little when he uses his other hand to pour us more wine. It's impossible for me to tell him that there's finally enough love inside me because that must also mean that he didn't fill me up to the brim, that there wasn't enough before.

What was our agreement, actually, I ask. We never made an actual agreement, he says, laughing. Wine drips on his shirt as he empties his glass.

The smoke machine is working again and artificial smoke mingles with cigarette smoke, hookah smoke, clouds of hash. We're both buzzing tonight. Our friends keep their distance, they can feel the sparks. I talk for a bit with one person, then another, resting my feet on a friend's legs and opening yet another beer, drinking without tasting. You're standing by the window, you throw a cigarette butt into the night sky. You keep an eye on me and I know that my red lipstick is not enough to divert your attention from my flickering eyes. Finally, you come over and kiss me on the neck, the mouth on the face next to me makes an O and says AAWW. A new face, with a ponytail, says: Why can't I have what you and Simon have? And I want to say be careful what you wish for. Electric blankets can ignite and we're burning now. You whisper something in my ear and goose bumps spread from my earlobe to my cheeks to my nipples to my calves. And then you're gone, but you come back. Your shirt is open and your T-shirt is black and clean. I washed it yesterday. I hung it up to dry, remembering to shake it so it wouldn't wrinkle drying on the rack.

Do you feel like a freak too?

I take your hand and pull you onto the dancefloor because we're both aliens and aliens have to dance with each other. No one else wants to dance with an alien. Everyone talks about them behind their backs, pointing at their antennas and webbed fingers, making fun of their bizarre way of being. Why does it feel like we're the losers? We're magicians. We're liars, but we're honest too. Our dancing is hesitant at first, it's always hesitant at first for us. We were hesitant the first time we danced with each other, as if we didn't dare to jump into a coordinated moonwalk routine. You fiddle with the phone attached to the speaker. Its light makes your hair look transparent and white. You're half-hidden behind the speaker when the song starts:

One two three, one two three drink.

No one's hesitating anymore, no one's holding themselves back, we're not hesitating anymore, we're not holding ourselves back. Your arms are my chandelier and I swing from it, you spin me around, the dance floor empties, because the losers are dancing, and our hands, arms, legs and feet are everywhere. You hit one of the fleeing guests in the side of the head and don't apologise. Get out of here, tonight the dance floor belongs to the losers! You're a party boy and no one can touch you. Why aren't you wearing mascara on your eyelashes tonight? You're wearing my sequined trousers and they fit you perfectly. They're too big on me, but they're perfectly tight around your thighs, and the smoke hovers between the sequins like specks of dust, and they're the most beautiful trousers. We swallow MDMA in the bathroom. We don't lock the door behind us and you pee, the stream of urine is loud against the porcelain, and I watch and almost fall over, and you don't wash your hands because it doesn't matter. The bacteria are working on your hands just like our dance is working towards destruction. We are glittering and tonight is our night, this is our night. Back to the smoke, back in your arms, and Rihanna says that diamonds are forever, and we're the best losers in the universe.

Until we're not anymore. The music stops, the smoke machine coughs and we have to go home because we always have to go home when the night is over. And tomorrow we won't be dancing anymore because tomorrow the dance floor is only for winners. But we can't leave yet. We find a box of wine under the coffee table and fill up a few empty beer cans with wine because all the glasses are broken or have turned into ashtrays, and we sit there on the red velour sofa with a few friends between us. They stare at us as we laugh hollowly and loudly, we can't stop laughing. I can hear our laughter echoing between the walls. Our friends are worried. I can see it in their eyes. They're surrounded by aliens and they don't know how to escape. They ask us about being open, whether it really works, whether the honesty doesn't hurt more, and we don't answer. We laugh: HA. HAHA. As if that's an answer in itself. Are we still the same people? Toke enters the living room and sees the box of wine on the table and says that we should head home, and there's a tenderness in his eyes, and I want to hit him because he's not allowed to feel bad for us, no one's allowed to feel bad for us. We've got it all sorted out, doesn't he know that?

We fall asleep as soon as we get home. You don't take off the sequined trousers. When we wake up the next morning, our sheets are covered in black sequins, glittering in the dingy grey cotton duvet.

It's the first day of the month and I've been paid, Simon has deposited his *dagpenge*, Toke his *kontanthjælp* cheque. We buy a bottle of German champagne in Aldi to mix with orange juice, which we drink out of large water glasses with white streaks of calcium. Dina hasn't deposited anything. Her stipend was delayed because of some mix-up. We lend her some money that we know is a donation and not a loan.

There are prams on the green path and parents carrying their babies. Snot-nosed kids are playing in the sandbox, sand sticking to their palms and cheeks. We buy coffees from Ricco's that we can't afford. Maybe we should have a baby. It's Simon who says it and suddenly we're two parents walking with a child in between us. The child separates us, gives us the space we need, and Toke has to move out to make room for the cot. Simon paints the room a pretty shade of blue and the playground and its flag with the building's logo on it suddenly has a purpose. I don't mind that I have to walk crouched over to get to the laundry room anymore.

But both of us know that there won't be a cot. We won't go to Røverkøb to buy paint. Both of us know that we're keeping count of the days to my next period and both of us have googled how to get an abortion. And we know how painfully simple it is. At least it's something that Alexander and Simon look alike, Dina says. But I think that their eyes are different. I would like to see the difference on a second-trimester sonogram. To see the foetus winking at me. Would it be Simon's or Alexander's wink?

Simon puts on a song by Gavin DeGraw. He sings along, screaming so loud it echoes between the walls:

Your favourite fruit is chocolate covered cherries and seedless watermelon, oh, nothing from the ground is good enough!

You're just like her, he says gleefully, grabbing another orange wedge off the plate. You don't like the real thing, you only eat processed foods. It's suffocatingly hot in the flat, and the big windows are like magnifying glasses. We're ants and our public housing complex is holding a magnifying glass over us with childish fingers, watching us wriggle in the warmth, slowly turning sluggish. We smoke cigarettes and drink lukewarm mint tea and Toke peels more oranges. He keeps peeling until there aren't any more. Carefully he assembles a tower of orange wedges.

I can't eat peeled oranges. I like to eat them out of the peel so I can avoid as much of the white part as possible. I can't handle the bitter taste of the white strings, the artificial texture of white skin on my tongue. It's best to fill your mouth with a slice and suck. Suck out the juice and throw the rest in the bin, let the scraps rot with the plastic containers and coffee filters, the empty packs of cigarettes.

You're like a petulant child, Simon laughs, and I want to disagree with him, but there's no point because he's more accurate than he knows. He thinks he's talking about my eating habits, but it's about so much more – it's about everything. Peeled oranges aren't enough for me. Living the life I'm supposed to isn't enough for me either, with the master's degree and full-time job and townhouse and kids.

I used to hate the sandbox as a kid. I would spend the whole day on the swings trying to reach the clouds with the tips of my toes. It was a lonely kind of freedom. Following the rise and fall of the swing, the squeaky chains, my blurred field of vision. The playground disappeared and only the sky and the tips of my toes remained. My body disappeared and my trouser legs, my navel and little nipples were dissolved in blue. I remember that brief moment of weightlessness. I miss those weightless seconds in the sky.

I read online that the white part of the orange is called the albedo or the pith and that it's the healthiest part of the orange. I never want the healthy part; a personality trait I'd rather not dwell on.

Mathilde avoids me after Sunday afternoon, after Sunday night. We speak to each other at work. She says she'll make some more coffee and that she can answer my calls when I'm on my break. She hasn't worn the gold shoes since. Her black boots signal that it's over. At the end of the day, we leave without saying goodbye – she cycles past me and raises her arm in a half-hearted wave, and I cry. I cry again on Simon's chest later that night, and he strokes my hair and tells me that Mathilde isn't being fair. She doesn't understand what a good friend she's giving up. And I want to tell him that Mathilde isn't my friend, but I don't know whether or not that's true, so I just blow my nose and keep crying. I can feel his grin so wide it pulls at the skin on his chest. You're back! he rejoices the next morning when I open my eyes, I know those eyes!

I'm not back. I'm gone.

And then she finds me again. Effortless and graceful as only she can be. She sends me a red heart, and the message reaches my phone – new message from Mathilde – and when I open it, the screen is flooded at last with red, bubbling hearts exploding into little pixels and the sound of balloons popping. Her neck looks like it's made of marble as she bends over the printer. The door between the office and the print room is slightly ajar and I have to hold my desk to keep myself from running to her, kissing her neck until it turns soft and malleable. The phone rings. A customer hasn't received his delivery and I can't answer his question. I can only hear the sound of exploding heart bubbles on my phone and hang up: I apologise for the inconvenience. I'll look into it right away. Have a nice weekend.

It's only Monday, but inside me it's the weekend already. I send Mathilde my heart in a text message and I can see that she's received it. Read 15:30.

Do you want to go for a beer?

We sit down at a café with outdoor seating, only because the sky is too blue to justify the darkness of a brown bar. We find a table in the corner, the right corner. The pigeons can't reach us there. They land on the table next to ours, attacking half-eaten plates of nachos, shitting on the seat cushions and scaring away a group of teenagers, teenagers with mobile phones in their hands and insecurity in their mouths. Their voices like musical glasses. They screech as the pigeons approach, fleeing to another table. We smile, amused. We drink our beers. My phone goes off in my bag, and I let it vibrate. Mathilde's trembling body is hypnotising, and I swing between her and the bar, between her white spring jacket and the waiters' grey-blue polos. The alcohol settles like a membrane over our eyes, but we'll keep drinking until we're almost blind. That's the only way we can be together.

Alexander parks his bicycle against a tree on the other side of the street. He doesn't look in our direction until after he's locked his bicycle and we both observe him in silence. We don't dare look at each other before he's pulled over a chair from the next table. He sits down and the starter pistol is fired. Mathilde starts.

There's something I should apologise for.

Alexander knows what she's going to say. His feverish grasp around the beer bottle gives him away. He peels off the label and fumbles for a cigarette in his jacket pocket. I watch

Mathilde's mouth move, hearing the tinkling teenage voices instead, their babbling, something about a biology test, and she says:

Are you listening to what I'm saying?

Sorry, can you repeat that, I ask, and Mathilde apologises for her anger, for her inability to put her own needs aside. Sorry for being so jealous, she says. I was awake that Sunday night, she says. I was furious, I was breathing like crazy because I was so angry, and you didn't even notice, or you just didn't want to. Then her tone changes. Her voice is soft and without looking at Alexander, I can see him nodding along. Like a parent making their child apologise for excluding another kid at school. Can you say sorry to the little girl? Doing as he says doesn't suit her, but I would have done the same thing. I'm doing the same thing: I accept her apology, and we're all quiet.

Aren't you going to apologise too?

Mathilde doesn't say it, but her jaw is tensed, her mouth a little open in disappointment. I think about them disappearing in the taxi and it's impossible to apologise. I can't let them win this battle, even though it's two against one. I underestimated you, she says. I won't do that again. Let's try to move on, let's start with a clean slate, she says. I want

139

to be better – the project won't work if I'm jealous and possessive about Alexander. I've known for a while, but it's just hard to live up to.

But it's not about your project, Mathilde, I want to say. It's about love, and if you're jealous, that must mean you love me. That's the only explanation. Let's forget about the project. Let's go to Škofja Loka and be surrounded by Tomažes who will pay for our coffee and beer and cigarettes. We can walk through the city holding hands and we won't be foreigners. We'll have each other. But I don't say it because she leans forward and kisses me. I've missed her tongue and her smooth front teeth. She leans back, breaking off the kiss, even though my lips try to hold onto hers.

Simon's mother has decorated the tables with purple paper tablecloths and vases full of white flowers. The serviettes are purple too, but a shade darker, and they match her floor-length dress, shimmering in various hues of purple. She likes to be the hostess. It's clear in meticulously arranged place settings with two wine glasses and two forks, two knives, a single spoon. The handwritten table cards and candles on the windowsill. Simon is making gin & tonics. He sets them down on the buffet table, and all of a sudden she's standing right there: Can you make three even rows? This one needs more tonic. The guests arrive and they all resemble her with their greying hair and practical footwear and dresses with round necklines. They ask for another drink and find their places at the table. Give too-long speeches, show each other pictures from when they were young and shout *hurrah*. Three short and one long in the Danish tradition.

Wouldn't it be wonderful if you were my daughter-in-law!

Simon's mum slurs her words as she pulls me onto the

dance floor. We sway together for a bit, she's not moving in time to the music. She's too drunk to hear the thumping bass. It's just so easy with you two, she says. I can feel how happy you make each other. I pull out a chair for her. She sits down and asks for another glass of wine. Simon is scooping coffee into the machine in the kitchen. He pulls me to him, kisses me on the mouth with loose lips. Your mum likes us, I say, and he kisses me again. Spins me around until my plait hits my shoulder.

I want to go home.

Simon's mum pays for a cab because the last train has already left and Simon's hand rests on my knee. The cab stops at one red light and then the next. We drink white wine on the balcony – Simon stole a bottle from the party – and we talk about the party guests, the speeches, the purple table-cloths. I love you, he says, and I repeat his words and mean them. Do we have any beer, I ask, but Simon wants to go to bed. He's exhausted from all the talk and cheers and hurrah, and we fling ourselves into bed. He wraps me in the duvet, gives me a kiss on the forehead and closes his eyes.

I'm in love with Mathilde.

Simon's breathing is deep and slow. Maybe he doesn't hear me.

The housing association agreed to transfer the lease to me. Simon took care of everything. He submitted the exemption application and called the main office to explain our situation. They agreed to make an exception. He printed out a copy of the lease, it was sitting on the dining table one morning. I signed it with a blue pen, turned the stack of papers over with the blank side up.

He had bought a new apartment on Nordre Fasanvej. It was a good deal, a steal, because he knew someone who knew someone, and the owner wanted to sell the apartment as soon as possible – the price was negotiable, so long as Simon could move in straight away. I can definitely do that, he said on the phone, that's no problem at all, and I curled up on the bathroom floor, crying without tears on the white tiles. I heard the door slam, the keys jangling as he locked the door behind him. When I came home from work the next day, all of his things were gone. The hangers were naked on the clothes rack, the rug had left an outline of dust on the living room floor, and there were no more mugs in the kitchen cabinet. The green mugs were his too. He decided to leave his books because I had combined them with mine when we moved in together. Back then it didn't matter which book belonged to whom. We should put them in alphabetical order, he said, and I pulled up his T-shirt to warm my hands on his stomach, opening his belt and stroking the edge of his boxer shorts with teasing fingers.

He left his slippers here. They're in the hallway, one a little in front of the other, as if he disappeared mid-step.

Let's throw a party!

We need to celebrate your new beginning, Dina says, and she tries to make her voice sound light and easy, but the effort and concern is visible in the corners of her mouth. She opens a bottle of white wine and fills our glasses. White wine can fix anything, she says, patting my head. She wraps a blanket around her legs and sits down, turning her face towards the sun and closing her eyes, smiling contentedly. Toke waves from inside the living room. We can see him through the window. We're sitting on the balcony and Simon's books are watching us from the bookcase in the living room and I know that I'll have to rush past them when I go to the bathroom in a second. But I can't hold it anymore. Toke doesn't look up when I walk past. He's sitting on the sofa with his computer.

Dina and Toke are snuggled up on the sofa. She gives him a kiss on the cheek. Alice is going to have a party tomorrow, she says smiling at me, and Toke looks at me for a bit with an expression that I can't make out, maybe this is just how he's going to look at me from now on. Maybe it's disappointment, maybe it's powerlessness. Dina gives Toke another kiss on the cheek, and he says that sounds nice, but he doesn't want to intrude. Why don't you go out on the balcony, he says.

Dina grabs my phone and writes an invitation to send to my university friends, my high school friends, and also to a few of her friends who I just have to meet. You need to widen your social circle, she says and presses send. She drops her cigarette and bends down to pick it up, and there's my chance. I grab the phone and add Mathilde and Alexander to the group and feel the greed working itself through my body. I regret it immediately. We finish the bottle and soon my phone starts going off, messages are streaming in. A lot of people can come, some will come later. Emojis in every message: glasses of beer and bottles of champagne and hearts and stars. My ears are ringing, I can't hear what Dina is saying. I can only hear the pinging sounds from my phone. Every ping pierces my face like a needle, I can feel the needles in my nose, my cheeks, my eyebrows. And then Dina's voice breaks through, squealing: Everyone is coming! She spreads her arms wide to give the whole world a hug and I don't know why she doesn't just give me a hug instead.

I find some old linens in the closet and we use them as table-cloths to cover the shabby picnic tables in the court-yard. We place folded blankets on the benches for when the sun goes down. The first guests arrive and they come bearing gifts, even though it's not my birthday, and I take them, snip the ribbon and tear off the wrapping paper. I say thank you for the book and thank you for the gift card. Weren't you just saying you needed one of those? one of my friends asks, and I nod, say thank you and nod again. The flag with its logo is hanging limply on the pole. There's no wind and it's stiflingly warm and muggy. I lick the sweat off my upper lip. The taste of salt settles on the back of my tongue and I can't get rid of it.

I can't stop looking at the gate. I jump a little every time I hear the sound of a laugh or beer bottles clinking. I'm ready, ready to be hugged by Simon, and I imagine him coming home, opening the gate, running his hand through his hair that's a little too long. He stops on the lawn, takes a deep breath, and I get up, slide my feet into my sandals, and I start running. I fall into his arms and press my face against his chest, feeling it rising and falling, first fast, then slower. I'm home. At last, I'm home. And all the party guests clap and hoot, shouting over each other: I knew it! Those two will be together forever. But we weren't forever and Simon never arrives. The gate remains closed. His slippers are still there, abandoned in the hallway, and I squeeze my eyes tightly shut. Even the slightest glimmer of light could make me fall apart on this bench right now.

And then the gate slams. I open my eyes and Mathilde and Alexander are making their grand entrance. The queen has arrived. She kisses the people she knows on the cheek and disperses compliments like gold coins thrown to the masses. My friends are transformed into submissive subjects, bowing and curtseying. The queen and Alexander sit down on either side of me. There wasn't any extra room on the bench before but there is now, and Mathilde is wearing a pair of big black sunglasses, even though the sun has almost set. Alexander gets up again. He wants to go and buy some more beers, leaving us alone on the bench. There's only her. My Mathilde. Right now she's mine. But my face is reflected in her sunglasses and in their dark glass I see what she sees: a lost little girl with chapped lips and lonely eyes. My obsession is like a milky white membrane over my eyes. Who could love such a silly little girl?

Mathilde strokes my neck and lets her hand linger while she gossips with my friends, answering their questions: Yes, that's me. I'm Mathilde from the office. Her hand is so cold, so cold. The coolness makes my neck stiff and sore and I can feel my cunt contract.

What happened with Simon?

She asks with her head tilted, letting her hand slide from my neck down to my lower back, rubbing a little back and forth, resting it there. I'm in love with someone else, I say, and she withdraws her hand. She asks Alexander to get her another beer. I search her face but I can only see my own lost reflection, and she shakes her head, exhaling into the mouth of the bottle, and it lets out a low-pitched whistle. It feels like she's blowing into my mouth instead of the bottle. Her breath expands my lungs like a balloon, but I'm heavier than ever. And then she leans back, on the verge of falling off the bench. Her eyes disappear upwards and she opens her mouth, letting out a sigh:

Oh, Alice!

All of a sudden she wants to go home. The show is over and she grabs her bag from under the table, letting the pack of cigarettes fall into her pocket. She almost leaves her lighter behind, but remembers at the last second. She leans over the table, barely able to reach the lighter with her fingertips. Her sleeve brushes my cheek and then she's gone.

Alexander turns up the music. We drink the last of the beer and I fetch the rum. Simon left that behind too because it was a gift to the both of us from his mother. We drink it from the bottle as the party guests disappear like clouds dissolving in the night.

Louder!

The music can't get loud enough, we twirl around on the lawn, round and round we go, and I step on a piece of broken glass and want to cry. I sit down in the grass and try to find the shard of glass in the ball of my foot, but I can't see anything in the dark. The skin of my feet is crumpled from the cold grass. Alexander is still standing, bending over me. He puts a hand on my head and asks what's wrong. Don't you understand, I ask, looking up at him.

I'm in love with someone else.

Alexander doesn't need to hear her name. His face changes, his pupils expand, and he takes his hand away from my head. He stands in front of me and grabs my hands, helping me to my feet. We almost stumble over each other's legs. Let's go to the playground, he says, and I wobble behind him.

The hinges squeak. I pull hard and extend my legs. Soon I'll be able to reach the clouds with my toes. I just need a little more speed, to extend my legs a little more in the gentle ascent, and then I'll be able to reach the sky. Alexander is sitting silently on the swing next to me. He lights a cigarette and smokes it slowly. And then the sky opens. The rain patters against the roof of the bicycle shed. Alexander throws his cigarette on the ground. I open my mouth and the drops land on my tongue. I can feel the rush in my stomach and I'm a kid again. Back and forth, the rain picks up, and my curls surrender. They collapse and strands of hair cling to my cheeks, but I don't care. All I can do is swing.

The seat is still swaying back and forth behind us when Alexander spreads my legs and kneels between them. His black pupils make me want to say no, but my mouth is dry and closed. I have to breathe through my nose.

Can you stop.

I don't say it because I can't say anything. It's not only my mouth that's dry and closed. My whole body is dried out. The rain slides off me as if I've been doused in some kind of water-repellent spray, and I think about Mathilde's cold hand on my neck, the gate slamming shut behind her. Alexander's fingers are hard. He rips my zip open, my underwear is caught in it so he has to pull hard. He pushes my trousers down to my ankles and I try to push his head away but his hair is too slithery and I let my arms fall to my sides, feel the gravel through my sleeves, hear it crunching.

Please, stop.

He spits in his hands and rubs my clitoris with a new kind of force, massaging until I'm wet, and then he pulls my labia aside, the folds are pulled apart. When he pushes into me, his hands wrap around my neck and turn my face to the sky. He closes his eyes from the rain and I shut mine too. The swaying swings disappear, his groans disappear, the rain drops on my cheeks. Only Mathilde's pale hands remain. She waves me over from the bar at Café Intime and Alexander keeps thrusting.

And then it's over. Mathilde's waving hand and Alexander's groans. It's all over and he collapses on top of me. I can feel his breath on my neck. His large coat encloses us. Beyond the dark windows, families are asleep in their flats. If a sleepless parent were to look down into the courtyard right now, we would probably look like a pile of clothes, left behind by someone on the playground.